"You told me to live," she whispered, slipping her tongue between his lips.

"I am living. This is what I want. Love me. *Love me!*" she continued.

Her own body was so aroused that she wondered how it could still obey her. But then she was operating on instinct. And love.

Cassian tore his mouth away, his face strained. "But afterward—"

"Forget afterward. This is now," she said fiercely.

The ecstasy in her body was nothing to the joy in her head, her heart and her soul. Cassian would possess her.

MISTRESS
TO A
MILLIONAIRE

Sara Wood

THE UNEXPECTED MISTRESS

MISTRESS
TO A
MILLIONAIRE

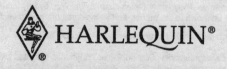

HARLEQUIN®

TORONTO • NEW YORK • LONDON
AMSTERDAM • PARIS • SYDNEY • HAMBURG
STOCKHOLM • ATHENS • TOKYO • MILAN • MADRID
PRAGUE • WARSAW • BUDAPEST • AUCKLAND

ISBN 0-373-12263-2

THE UNEXPECTED MISTRESS

First North American Publication 2002.

Visit us at www.eHarlequin.com

Printed in U.S.A.

CHAPTER ONE

CASSIAN lounged contentedly on the roof of the large rented house which he shared in typically cosmopolitan style with two English strippers, a Buddhist from Florida, and a Moroccan herbalist. It was late, the sky a dense black scattered with stars, the air warm and still.

He and his literary agent were watching the snake charmers and acrobats performing in the *Djemaa el Fna*, Marrakesh's extraordinary market square. His agent's mouth had been almost permanently open since they'd emerged onto the roof ten minutes ago and Cassian's dark eyes hadn't stopped twinkling in gentle amusement.

'A tad different from central London,' his agent marvelled with great understatement, goggling at a group of Saharan nomads who were sweeping majestically through the square.

Men in rags, walking like kings, Cassian thought, reflecting on his belief that outer trappings often concealed the real person beneath.

'Same world. Different values and desire. Life stripped to its bare necessities. The need to eat, to find shelter and love,' he observed lazily.

Stirred but not staggered by the scene below, Cassian poured coffee from the silver beaked pot and offered his agent a sweet pastry. After living here for a year, it had all become gloriously familiar to him; the huge lanterns illuminating the storytellers, the contortionists, the clowns and boy dancers, and the crowd of Berbers mingling with an incongruous sprinkling of awestruck tourists.

By now his ears were attuned to the din. Drums, cymbals and western music drowned the hubbub of voices—and

5

also, mercifully, the groans coming from the stall of the dentist who was enthusiastically wielding his pliers.

A willing slave to intense feelings and sensuality, Cassian delightedly inhaled the powerful aroma of humanity mingling with spices and the smell of cooking from the blazing braziers dotted around the square. And he wondered curiously where his passion for living life to the hilt would take him next.

'So,' said his agent in bright cocktail-speak, clearly uncomfortable with the culture shock he was experiencing. 'Now you've finished the book, I suppose you and your son are both going home for a while?'

Cassian sipped his Turkish coffee, appreciating its richness. 'Jai and I have no home,' he said gravely.

And yet... As if to contradict that statement, an image had come unexpectedly into his mind. Instead of the black night and the ochre buildings, the blazing torches and the patchwork of bright colours below, he saw emerald-green hills laced with grey stone walls, ancient woodlands and small stone villages by a cool, rushing river. The Yorkshire Dales. And, specifically, Thrushton.

Astonished, he inhaled deeply as if he could feel the freshness of the champagne air in his lungs. For the first time in his life he felt a pang of longing for a place he'd once known and loved.

That startled him: he who'd spent his adult life passionately embracing a setting, teasing out its darker side to create one of his popular thrillers...and then leaving without regret for new sensations, new horizons.

'Still, you must have a great sense of relief,' his agent persisted. 'You've got your freedom back, for a start. No more sitting hunched over a PC for hour after hour,' he added jovially, attempting to penetrate the mysterious psyche of the man he knew only as Alan Black.

'I never lose my freedom. If I ever felt it was threatened,' Cassian replied quietly, 'I'd stop writing at once.'

'Hell, don't do that! We've got another film producer offering us an option on your next book!' panicked his agent, seeing twelve per cent of a fortune vanishing overnight.

But Cassian had stopped listening. His sharp ears had heard an unusual noise in the narrow alley beside the house. Moving to the low parapet, he could see a man there, curled up in a foetal position and moaning with pain. Someone was running into the darkness of the souk beyond. Without making a fuss, he politely excused himself and went to investigate.

It was a few minutes before he realised that the bruised and battered man he'd hauled into the house was Tony Morris, his old enemy from that very part of England which had sprung to mind so surprisingly at the mention of the word 'home'.

As Tony blubbered and whimpered, and he silently washed the blood from the flabby face, Cassian found his longing for Yorkshire increasing quite alarmingly, the memories coming hot and fast and extraordinarily insistent.

Ruled by his instincts, he acknowledged that perhaps it was time to go back. Time to immerse himself in the landscape which had reached like loving arms into his unhappy soul and given him solace and peace of mind. Time also to face the devils that haunted his dreams.

And then Tony offered him the opportunity on a plate to do just that.

Laura slammed two mugs on the table and doled out the last of the coffee granules with a preoccupied expression. Coffee wasn't the only thing she'd have to eliminate from her shopping list. Poverty was staring her in the face.

'Sue,' she said urgently to her life-long friend, 'I've got to get a new job sharpish.'

Sue looked sympathetic. 'Nothing yet, then?'

'No. *And* I've been searching in Harrogate all this week!'

'Wow!' Sue exclaimed, suitably impressed.

Her friend was the only person who knew what a huge step that had been. It was a month now since she'd lost her job. Night after night, Laura had lain awake worrying about her child's future, his poor health, his fragile state of mind. For Adam's sake she *must* find work! She must! she'd thought with increasing panic.

No work was available in Thrushton where she lived, nor in the small community of Grassington nearby. None, either in nearby Skipton.

Up to now her entire existence had been confined to the rolling dales and picturesque stone villages surrounding the River Wharfe. Of the rest of Yorkshire, she knew nothing— let alone England—and the thought of travelling further to work had made her blanch with apprehension.

It was a stupid reaction, she knew, but not one of her making. If she had ever been born with self-assurance and confidence, then it had been crushed by her restrictive up- bringing. If she'd ever had ambition then that too had with- ered and died, thanks to the critical tongue of her adoptive father's sister, Aunt Enid, and the scorn and cruelty of her father's son Tony.

She knew she was submissive and reticent to a fault. But the needs of her own child meant a radical rethink of her life. It didn't matter to *her* that she wore jumble sale clothes, but she had to earn good money and buy some decent gear for Adam—or he'd continue to be bullied un- mercifully.

'I'd do anything,' she said fervently, 'to ensure we can stay here. This house is my...my...'

'Comfort blanket,' supplied Sue with a grin. 'Be honest. It is.'

Laura glared at her horribly perceptive friend and then let her tense mouth soften in recognition.

'You're right. But I need stability and familiarity in my life. Adam too. We'd both go to pieces anywhere else.'

'I know, duck. I think you've got real grit to pluck up the courage to hunt for work in Harrogate.' Raising a plump arm, Sue patted Laura's long and elegant hand in admiration. 'But…it'd be a bit of a nightmare journey without a car, wouldn't it?'

Laura grimaced. 'Two buses and a train and a long walk. What choice do I have, though? Nine-year-old boys can eat for England. Mind you, employers weren't exactly falling over themselves to take me on. I'm fed up! I've exhausted every avenue,' she complained crossly.

'Must be *some*thing out there,' Sue encouraged.

Laura rolled her eyes. 'You bet there is. Lap dancing.'

Tension made her join in with Sue's giggles but it was frustrated resentment that made her jump up and perform a few poses around an imaginary pole. She adopted an 'I am available' face and moved her body with sinuous grace. It seemed an easy way to earn money.

'Crikey. I'd give you five quid!' Sue said admiringly. 'Madly erotic. But then you've got the most fab legs and body. That monumentally baggy shirt would have to go, though,' she advised. 'Wrong colour!'

Hastily smoothing her tousled hair, Laura subsided breathily into the chair and wriggled down her slim skirt— which she'd acquired like most of her clothes from the local jumble sale and which was almost a size too small.

She felt quite shaken by her erotic performance. She was a natural. Perhaps these things could be passed on genetically, she thought gloomily. After all, she was a bastard. That had been rammed into her enough times.

If only she knew what her real mother had been like! Then she wouldn't have to wonder if her mother *had* been a tart, as Aunt Enid had claimed.

'She was a slut!' Enid—her father's sister—had claimed. 'Your mother slept with anyone and everyone. And married to your father, a respectable solicitor! Diana brought the name of Morris into disrepute.'

Laura would never know the truth. Would never know why her mother had been unfaithful. Would never know the identity of her real father. Nobody else knew that she *wasn't* George Morris's child.

As soon as Laura was born, her mother had run away and George had had no choice but to bring Laura up as his daughter. Which he'd resented. That explained his indifference and total lack of affection.

Misty-eyed, she looked around the comfortable, stone-flagged kitchen with its huge Aga and deep inglenook fireplace, wincing as she imagined the uproar when her mother's infidelity had been discovered. And she understood how hard it must have been for her 'father' to accept his wife's bastard.

Together with Aunt Enid, he had created a regime so narrow and unbending in an effort to keep her on the straight and narrow, that she had turned into a timid mouse. Albeit, she thought wryly, with unrivalled domestic skills and a posture a ramrod would be proud of. Pity she didn't have other qualifications. She might be more employable.

'You know, Sue,' she confided, 'sometimes I've felt as though I'm *prostituting* myself at interviews with all that smiling, all that looking eager and charming and willing…oh, I hate it all!'

Close to losing control, she thumped the table, and Sue jumped in surprise at Laura's unusual vehemence.

'Something'll turn up,' her friend soothed, not very convincingly. 'I've got my dental appointment later, in Harrogate. I'll get the local paper for you to look through the Jobs Vacant column.'

'I'll do anything decent and legal. I'm willing to learn, conscientious and hard-working…but the downside is that I'm plain and shy and my clothes are out of the Ark,' Laura muttered. 'I see all the other applicants glowing with confidence in their make-up and attractive outfits and I know they're laughing at me behind their smooth, lily-white hands!' Glaring, she held up her own. 'Look at mine! They're rough enough to snag concrete. I tell you, Sue, I'd be just as good as them, given a lick of lippy, a decent haircut and a ten-gallon drum of hand cream!'

'I've never known you so forceful,' Sue marvelled.

'Well. It's because I'm angry.' Laura's blue eyes flashed with rare inner fire. 'When will the world recognise that appearances aren't everything? That it's what's here—' she banged her chest vigorously '—and here—' her head had the same treatment '—that's important! And what's that removal van doing outside?' she wondered, breaking off with a frown.

'Getting lost,' suggested Sue without interest. 'Nobody round here's moving that I know about.'

Built from local rock in the Middle Ages and enlarged in the Georgian period, Thrushton Hall stood at the far end of the twenty other stone houses that comprised the tiny village, a cheerful cottage garden separating the handsome manor house from the narrow lane outside—which led only to the river.

Laura leaned across the deep window embrasure and peered through the stone mullioned window. Clearly the van driver had missed a turning. And yet the name plaque on the low drystone wall seemed to satisfy the removal men who'd jumped from the cab, because they brought out a flask and sandwiches and proceeded to settle themselves on the wall to eat.

'Well, unknown to us, we've become a designated picnic spot!' Laura declared wryly. A battered four-wheel drive cruised up and drew to a halt behind the small van. 'Here's another picnicker!' she called back to her friend. 'Huh! We'll have a coachload of tourists here in a minute and I'll have to give them sun umbrellas, waste bins and loo facilities! Sue, come and…!'

But her words died in her throat. From the Range Rover

emerged a tall, slim figure in black jeans and T-shirt. The
breath left her lungs as if they'd been surgically deflated.

'What's the matter?' Sue hurried up, then grabbed
Laura's arm with a gasp. 'Blow me! Isn't that…?'

Laura's eyes had grown huge, her lashes dark against the
unnatural pallor of her face.

'Yes!' she choked. 'It's Cassian!'

His appearance was so unexpected, so utterly bizarre,
that she stood rooted to the ground in numb disbelief while
he chatted to the men. And then he began to turn to the
house. Like children caught doing something naughty, she
and Sue hastily dodged back out of sight.

'What a hunk he's become!' Sue declared. 'He's absolutely scrummy. But…why's he here—of all places?!'

Laura couldn't speak at all. Her mind was whirling, confused by the sight of the dark and sinister figure, whose
sudden arrival seventeen years ago—and equally sudden
disappearance five years later—had split her family apart.

She'd been ten at the time. Her father had begun to talk
of nothing but a female client who'd come to his legal
practice. One day he had announced that he was to marry
the artist he'd been defending—and that his bride and her
twelve-year-old son would be moving in. It was only then
that Laura had realised George must have divorced her
mother.

Tony, up till then the adored and spoilt only son, had
been scarlet with fury at the news. For her, the arrival of
Bathsheba and Cassian had been a revelation. Suddenly the
house had burst into life with colour and laughter and music
and Laura had quickly become familiar with the smell of
turpentine mingling with that of the herbs and spices of
exotic dishes.

But almost immediately there had been titanic rows over
Cassian's behaviour. Laura could see him now; a silent and
glowering boy who couldn't behave conventionally and
who'd refused to fit into the community.

Vividly she recalled his defiance in the face of Aunt Enid's rigid rules and the way he'd disappeared for days, seemingly existing without food or comfort.

And while she'd envied his independence and stubborn refusal to be anyone other than himself, she'd feared that very freedom he exemplified. He had been untameable, with an adventurous, bohemian past and he came from a greater world than she or her friends could ever know or understand.

And so they were strangers to one another. She had admired and watched him from afar, wishing she had his nerve, envying his daring.

As he had grown into a young man, the depth of his inner assurance had attracted the girls like bees to a honeypot. He was the local Bad Boy, and women longed to be noticed by him. One or two were. The chosen dazed and dazzled girls had huddled in Grassington square, discussing with awe the passion they'd unwittingly unleashed, while she'd listened in horror.

And, she was ashamed to say, with a secret excitement. Not that she'd want to be part of his life at all. He scared her though she didn't know why, and she couldn't fathom what made her heart race whenever she set eyes on him.

It was quickening now, bringing a flush to her cheeks. Squirming with dismay, she took a cautious peek out of the window. Cassian had resumed talking to the removal men, one foot on the low wall, an expressive hand gesticulating as he described something.

A strange exhilaration caught hold of her, something that coiled warm and throbbing in her veins. She stared, mesmerised. Cassian had charisma. He had always been different, magnetic, special.

Laura shot a glance at Sue. Even her sensible, down-to-earth friend was gazing open-mouthed at him, her expression nakedly admiring. And Sue was in a state of tension, her fingers gripping the curtain tightly.

Just as she was, Laura thought in surprise, releasing the
creased curtain in embarrassment. She didn't like being disturbed like this and she felt uncomfortable that her nerves
were jiggling about all over the place.

Why should he make her pulses leap about so erratically?
It didn't make sense. Oh, he was good-looking enough in
a foreign kind of way. Handsome, she supposed. But so
were many other men who'd walked into the hotel where
she'd worked: young, affluent and personable, and she'd
been indifferent to them. And they to her, of course!

Bemused, she scrutinised him carefully in an effort to
solve the mystery. And felt her fascination go up a notch
or two. His hair was still dark—black and gleaming with
the richness of a raven's wing—but it was shorter now, the
rebellious curls sleekly hugging the beautiful shape of his
head.

His face... Well, those high cheekbones and carved jaw
would make any woman's heart beat faster coupled with
the dark, intense eyes and sexily mobile mouth. She sup-
pressed a small quiver in her breast.

'What's he doing?' hissed Sue.

'Don't know.'

Her voice had been hoarse because his liquid and relaxed
gestures had caused the muscles to ripple beneath his black
T-shirt in a way that left her breathless.

'He's beautifully toned,' Sue whispered, eyes agog. 'Not
over-developed—just perfect. Wow! And he used to be so
skinny.'

No, Laura wanted to say. He was always strong and wiry.
But she didn't want to betray her ridiculously chaotic hormones by speaking. His shoulders and chest had certainly
expanded. Cassian's torso was now a devastatingly attractive triangle of powered muscle and sinew.

She watched him, her eyes wide and puzzled. He was
more than just a perfect body. He...

She stiffened, suddenly realising what drew her to him.

Cassian possessed what she—and many others—might search for all their lives. Something that money couldn't buy. Total self-assurance.

She let out her tightly held breath. Cassian was sublimely at home in his own skin, whereas she had lived in the shadow of someone else's rules and had moulded her behaviour to the will of others. She was someone else's creation. He was his own.

And she longed to be like him.

Suddenly he laughed, and she felt a sharpness like a vice in her chest as she was almost bowled over by the sheer force of life which imbued his whole body—his brilliant white teeth flashing wickedly in the darkness of his face, the tilt of his chin, the warmth in those hot, dark eyes.

'Now that's what I call sex appeal!' Sue whispered in awe. 'Isn't he like his mother? What was her name?'

Laura swallowed and found a husky voice emerging. 'Bathsheba.'

'Unusual. Suited her.'

'Exotic,' Laura agreed.

His mother had been the most beautiful and vibrant woman she'd ever known. Bathsheba had dark, wavy hair, eyes that flashed like scimitars when she was happy, and a face with the same classically chiselled bones as Cassian's.

For the five years that Bathsheba had been her stepmother, neither she nor Cassian had taken much notice of her. But then Enid had kept them apart as much as possible.

And tragically, during the time that Bathsheba and her father were together, Laura had witnessed how two people could love one another but be incapable of living with one another. They were torn asunder by their differing views—particularly where the disciplining of Cassian was concerned.

'Bathsheba and Cassian vanished overnight, I remember,' Sue mused.

Laura nodded. 'They *walked* out into the night, taking

nothing with them! I was appalled. I wondered where
they'd live, how they'd cope. George never recovered, you
know.'

Her eyes softened. It seemed incredible that one person
could have such an effect on another. Her stern, unbending
father had died of a broken heart. She shivered, shrinking
from the destructiveness of passion. In her experience, it
had never done anyone any good.

'Well, Cassian's got over his feelings about Thrushton.
He's coming up the path!' Sue marvelled. 'Oh, why does
something riveting like this have to happen, when I'm going on holiday tomorrow?!'

Laura couldn't believe her eyes. 'He's hardly likely to
stay long. He hated this house!' she said, feeling an irrational sense of panic. 'This can't be a social call. He never
noticed me, hardly knew I existed. And he just loathed
Tony—'

She gasped. A key was rattling in the lock. There was a
pause. Cassian must have realised that the kitchen door
wasn't locked at all. The latch was lifted. Laura couldn't
breathe. *Why did he have a key?*

The door creaked open a fraction. And then it was flung
back with considerable force.

In an instant, the room seemed to be filled with him,
with the blistering force of his anger. She cringed back
instinctively by the half-concealing fall of the curtain,
afraid of his potency and bewildered by the physical impact
he had on her.

Cassian simmered with a volcanic rage as he scanned the
kitchen with narrowed and glittering eyes. And all too soon,
the full force of his incandescent fury became focussed directly at her.

CHAPTER TWO

THE smell of freshly baked bread had hit him immediately as he'd opened the door—even before it had swung fully open. Although his senses had enjoyed the aroma, he'd tensed every muscle in his body.

It meant one thing. A sitting tenant. And a legal minefield ahead.

Unsettled, he'd paused to collect himself. He had wanted to be alone here when he first arrived. To chase away the past. That was why he'd left Jai in Marrakesh, exploring the High Atlas mountains with one of their Berber friends.

Instead, it looked as if he'd have to chase a tenant out first! Furious with Tony for not mentioning that he'd rented the place out, he'd thrust at the door with an impatient hand and stepped into the room.

His heart had beat loud and hard as he'd entered the house where he'd cut his teeth on conflict, toughened his character and learnt to deal with Hell. He'd steeled himself.

And then he'd seen Laura.

The shock rocked him. It was a moment before he could collect his wits, a fearsome scowl marring his features and his eyes narrowing in disbelief as he realised the situation.

'You!' he growled, his voice deep with disappointment.

Of all people! She ought to have gone years ago, left this house and made a new start in life!

When she flinched, obviously struck dumb by his greeting, he scowled harder still, silently heaping vicious curses on Tony's fat head. Her huge eyes were already wary and reproachful. Instinctively he knew that she'd weep pathetically when he turned her out and he'd feel a heel.

'Hi, Cassian!'

17

He started, and glanced sideways in response to the cheery greeting from a strawberry blonde.

'Sue,' he recalled shortly and she looked pleased.

In a second or two he had assessed her. A ring. Biting into her finger. Married for a while, then. Weight increase from children or comfortable living—perhaps both. Her clothes were good, her hair professionally tinted.

She didn't interest him. He turned his gaze back to Laura, drawn by her mute dismay and her total stillness. And those incredible black-fringed eyes.

'W-what…are you doing here?' she stumbled breathily.

Cassian's mouth tightened, his brows knitted heavily with impatience. She didn't know! Tony had taken the coward's way out, it seemed, and not told his adopted sister what he'd done with the house he'd inherited on his father's death. Little rat! Selfish to the last!

'I gather Tony didn't warn you I was coming,' he grated.

Her lips parted in dismay and began to tremble. For the first time he realised they weren't thin and tight at all, but full and soft like the bruised petals of a rose.

'No!' She looked at him in consternation. 'I—I haven't heard from him for nearly two years!'

'I see,' he clipped.

The frightened Laura flicked a nervous glance at the removal van. Her brow furrowed in confusion and she bit that plush lower lip with neat white teeth as the truth apparently dawned.

'You're not…oh, no! No!' she whispered in futile denial, her hands restlessly twisting together.

And he wanted to shake her. It annoyed him intensely that she hadn't changed. This was the old Laura, self-effacing, timid, frightened. He did the maths. She'd been fifteen when he'd left. That made her twenty-seven now. Old enough to realise that she was missing out on life.

His scowl deepened and she shrank back as if he'd hit her, then with a muttered exclamation she whirled and frantically grabbed a tea towel, beginning to polish the hell out of some cutlery that was drying on the drainer. It was a totally illogical thing to do, but typical.

Cassian felt the anger remorselessly expanding his chest. His eyes darkened to black coals beneath his heavy brows.

She'd always been desperately cleaning things in an attempt to be Enid's little angel, not realising that she would never achieve her aim and she might as well cut loose and fling her dinner at the vicious old woman.

It appalled him that she hadn't come out of her shell. Well, she'd have to do just that, from this moment on.

'Just stop doing that for a moment.'

Grim-faced, he took a step nearer and she looked up warily, all moist-eyed and trembling.

'I—I need to!' she blurted out.

'Displacement therapy?' he suggested irritably.

Close up, he was surprised by the sweetness of her face. It was small and heart-shaped with sharply defined cheekbones and a delicate nose. Her rich brown hair looked nondescript and badly cut—though clean and shiny in the morning light which streamed through the window. His sharp senses picked up the scent of lavender emanating from her.

And signs of fear. Although her body was rigid, there was a tiny twitch at the corner of her mouth where she was trying to control a quivering lip. Perhaps she knew his arrival presented some sort of threat to her beloved security, he mused.

'I—I don't know what you mean!' she protested.

Her whole body had adopted a defensive pose. Arms across breasts. Shoulders hunched, eyes wary. He sighed. This wouldn't be easy.

'I realise this is a shock, me barging in, but I didn't expect to see anyone here,' he said gruffly, softening his voice a little without intending to.

'Tony gave you a key!' she cried, bewildered.

'That's right.'

'Why?'

He frowned. She'd sussed out the situation, hadn't she? 'To get in,' he said drily.

'But…'

He saw her swallow, the sweet curve of her throat pale against the faded blue of her threadbare shirt. Noticing his gaze, she blushed and put down the tea towel, her hand immediately lifting again to conceal the tatty collar.

His body-reading skills came automatically into use. Obviously she was poor. And she was proud, he noted. Slender hands, roughened from physical work. Pale face… Indoor work, then. She must be on night shifts—or out of a job, since she was home on a weekday.

Not married or engaged, no sign of a ring. But several pictures of a child in the room. Baby shots, a toddler, a school snap of a kid a bit younger than his own son. He felt intrigued. Wanted to learn more.

'I'm confused. That removal van…' She cleared her throat, her voice shaking with nerves. 'It can't…it doesn't mean that…that Tony has let you stay here with me?!' she asked in a horrified croak.

So that was what she'd thought. 'No. It doesn't. But—'

'Oh!' she cried, interrupting him. 'That's a relief!'

He was diverted before he could correct the conclusion she'd drawn. Laura's slender body had relaxed as if she'd let out a tense breath, the action drawing his eyes down to where her breasts might be hiding beneath the shirt which was at least two sizes too big.

Fascinated by her, he kept his investigation going and finished his scrutiny, observing the poor quality of her skirt and scuffed sneakers. Long legs, though. Slightly tanned, slender and shapely.

He felt a kick of interest in his loins and strangled it at birth. Laura wasn't his kind of woman. He adored women of all kinds, but he preferred them with fire coming out of their ears.

'Laura,' he began, unusually hesitant.

Sue jumped in. 'Hang on. If you haven't come to stay, why bring a removal van?' she asked in a suspicious tone.

'I'm about to explain,' he snapped.

He frowned at her because he didn't want her to be there. This was between him and Laura. Like it or not, Laura would have to go and he didn't want anyone else complicating matters when he told her the truth.

He'd tell her straight, no messing. Disguising the news with soft words wouldn't make a scrap of difference to the situation.

He sought Laura's wondering gaze again, strangely irritated by her quietly desperate passivity. She ought to be yelling at him, demanding to know what he was doing, persuading him to go and never return. But she meekly waited for the world to fall in on her.

He wanted to jerk her into life. To make her lose her temper and to see some passion fly. At the same time, he felt an overwhelming urge to protect her as he might protect a defenceless animal or a tiny baby. She was too vulnerable for her own good. Too easy to wound. Hell, what was he going to do?

In two strides he'd breached the distance between them. With the wall behind her, she had nowhere to go though he had the impression that she would have vanished through it if she could.

Grimly he took her arm, felt her quiver when he did so. Looking deeply into her extraordinary eyes, he saw that she recognised he was going to tell her something unpleasant.

'Sit down,' he ordered, hating the way she made him feel. Firmly he pushed her rigid body into the kitchen chair.

And inexplicably he kept a hand on her shoulder, intensely aware of its fragility, of the fineness of the bone structure of her face as she stared up at him in fear and apprehension, drowning him, making him flounder with those great big eyes.

'What is it?' she whispered.

Feeling distinctly unsettled by her, he dragged up a chair and sat close to her. Immediately she shrank away from him, covering her knees with her hands primly. His mouth tightened.

He loathed seeing her like this, a slave to her past, to the constant belittling by Enid which had relentlessly ground away her confidence. It had been just like the elements, the wind and the rain out there on the moors, grinding down solid rock over the years. She needed to leave. To find life. Her true self.

Confused by his own passionate views of Laura's future, he plunged in, eager to send her out into the world.

'When I said that I'm not staying here with you, Laura,' he said firmly, 'I meant that *you* won't be living here at all. I've bought Thrushton Hall from Tony. I'm moving in.'

'Moving...in?'

She was blinking, her eyes glazed over as if she didn't understand. He tried again so that there would be no mistake.

'Correct. You, Laura, will have to move out. Pronto.'

Laura let out a strangled gasp. Her stomach went into free fall, making her feel faint.

'No!' she whispered in pure horror. 'This is my home! All I've ever known! Tony wouldn't do that to me!'

'Yes, he would,' Sue muttered. 'He's a loathsome little creep.'

'That's true,' Cassian said in heartfelt agreement.

Laura stared at the implacable Cassian, her brain in a fog. 'This is ridiculous! I live here!'

'Not any more.'

She gave a little cry. 'I've been paying the bills and maintaining the house ever since Tony disappeared! You— you can't turn us out of here!' she said weakly.

'Us.'

Suddenly alert, he turned to scan the photographs around the room, his eyebrows asking an unspoken question.

'My son,' she mumbled, still dazed by Cassian's announcement. 'Adam,' she added blankly as tears of despair welled up in her eyes. 'He's nine.' She saw Cassian's eyes narrow, as he began to make a calculation and she jumped in before he could say anything. 'Yes, if you're wondering, I was eighteen when he was born!' she defied hysterically, bracing herself for some sign of disapproval.

Cassian, however, seemed unfazed. 'You and your son,' he said quietly. 'No one else living with you?'

Suddenly she wanted to startle him as he'd startled her. Panic and fear were making her unstable. A spurt of anger flashed through her and with uncharacteristic impetuosity she answered;

'I'm totally alone. I never *had* a husband—or even a partner!'

Everyone here knew how the travelling salesman from Leeds had flattered her by pretending she was beautiful. He must have seen a gauche, nervous and drab female in ill-fitting clothes and decided it would be easy for his silver tongue to dazzle her. Laura realised now that her transparent innocence, coupled with her teenage desperation to be loved, had been her downfall.

She flinched. There had been one fateful evening of bewilderment and repugnance—on her part—and then the arrival of Adam, nine months later. The shame of what she'd done would live with her for ever. And yet she had Adam, who'd brought joy to her dreary life.

Annoyingly, Cassian took her confession in his stride. 'I see,' he said non-committally.

Laura stiffened. 'No you don't!' she wailed. 'You stroll in here, claiming you've bought Thrushton Hall—'

'Want to see the deeds?' he enquired, foraging in the back pocket of his jeans.

The colour drained from her face when she saw the document he was holding out to her. Snatching it from him, she frantically unfolded it and read the first few lines, her heart contracting more and more as the truth sank in.

This was Cassian's house. She would have to leave. Her legs trembled.

'No! I don't believe it!' she whispered, aghast.

Despite the harshness of her childhood, this house held special memories. It was where her mother had lived. Deprived of any tangible memories of her mother, it comforted her that she walked in her mother's footsteps every day of her life. And Cassian intended to drive her away.

'You have no choice.'

Her head snapped up, sending her hair whirling about her set face. A frightening wildness was possessing her. Hot on its heels came an urge to lash out and pummel Cassian till his composure vanished and he began to notice her as a person instead of an irritating obstacle he needed to kick out of his way.

Her emotions terrified and appalled her. They seemed to fill her body, surging up uncontrollably with an evil, unstoppable violence. She fought them, groping for some kind of discipline over them because she didn't know what would happen if she ever allowed those clamouring passions to surface.

'You don't want this house! You can't possibly want to live here!' she whispered, hoarse with horror.

His calm, oddly warm eyes melted into hers.

'I do. I can.'

She took a deep, shuddering breath but she was losing a battle with her temper. Her child's security was threatened. She wouldn't allow that.

'This is my *home*!' she insisted tightly, clinging for dear life to the last vestiges of restraint. 'Adam's home!'

He shrugged as if homes were unimportant. 'I had the

impression that it was Tony's. Now it's mine. Do you pay rent?'

'N-no—'

'Then you have no legal rights to stay.'

Laura gasped, her hand flying to her mouth in consternation. 'Surely I do! I must have some kind of protection—'

'There could be an expensive legal case,' he conceded. 'But you'd have to go eventually. You'd save time and hassle if you did so straight away.' He smiled in a friendly way, as if that would console her. 'You'll find somewhere else. You might discover that moving from Thrushton turns out to be a good idea in the long run.'

She glared and was incensed when his eyes flickered with satisfaction. It was as if he welcomed her anger!

'What do you know?' she yelled. Dear heaven! she thought. She was losing control, acting like a banshee—and couldn't stop herself! 'It's a stupid idea! For a start, I don't have any money!' she choked, scarlet from the shameful admission. But he had to know her circumstances. 'There's nowhere I can go!' she cried in agitation. 'Nowhere I can afford!'

He continued to gaze at her with a steely eye, his heart clearly unmoved by her plight. And she knew that her hours in her beloved house—*his* house, she thought furiously—were probably numbered.

'It's true. She's dead broke. Lost her job,' confirmed Sue, suddenly butting in. Cassian jerked his head around in surprise as if he, like Laura, had forgotten Sue was there. 'I reckon she can stay put if she chooses—'

'I don't deny that.' Cassian flung an arm across the back of the chair, his eyes relentlessly fixed to Laura's. She flinched as his expression darkened, becoming unnervingly menacing. 'But you ought to know that living with me wouldn't be pleasant,' he drawled.

'Meaning?' Sue demanded.

He shrugged. 'I'd be…difficult.' His eyes seemed to be issuing a direct challenge. 'I'd eat her food, play music late at night, change the locks…' There was a provocative curve to his mouth, something…unnerving in his expression as his gaze swept her up and down. 'Laura, I'm not changing my way of living for anybody, and I have the distinct impression that you'd be shocked by the way I wander about half-naked after my morning shower, with just a small towel covering me and my—'

'Please!' she croaked.

'I'm just warning you,' he murmured with a shrug.

She felt hot. The rawness of his huge energy field reached out to enfold her in its greedy clasp and she instinctively flattened herself against the back of the chair.

She blushed, ashamed to be assailed by the unwanted rivulets of molten liquid which were coursing through her veins. His sexuality was too blatant, too unavoidable. This was something alien to her and she couldn't cope with it. Didn't want it at all. Living with him would be a nightmare.

'It's no use! I can't stay if he's living here!' she declared to Sue shakily. 'Sharing would be impossible!'

'Don't you give up!' Sue snapped. She glared at Cassian. 'Laura's been far too sheltered all her life to manage anywhere else—so you leave her alone, you ruthless, selfish brute. Push off back where you came from!'

Cassian rose, his eyes dark and glittering. 'I'm not going anywhere, whatever insults you choose to hurl at me. I'm moving in, once the removal men have finished their early lunch.'

'*Lunch?*' With a start, Sue glanced at the kitchen clock and let out a groan. 'Oh, crikey! My dental appointment! Never mind. I'll cancel it,' she offered urgently. 'You need backup, Laura—'

'No,' she said quickly, sick with nerves, hating the wobble in her voice.

This was her battle. Sue was making things worse.

Cassian had visibly tensed when Sue had shouted at him. He'd listen to logic, she was sure, but he wouldn't be bullied.

Proud and erect, she stood up with great dignity, conscious, however, that her five-seven didn't impinge on Cassian's six foot.

And they were now only inches apart, waves of heat thickening the space between them, pouring into her, the heavy, lifeless air clogging up her throat. Laura gulped, feeling that all the power was draining from her legs till they trembled from weakness.

'Well! Are you fighting me, Laura?' he taunted.

Rebellion drained away too when she met his challenging eyes. His confidence was daunting. How could she fight him when he held all the cards?

'I—I...'

'Still the mouse,' he mocked, but with a hint of regret in his dark regard. 'Still meekly huddling in the corner, afraid of being trodden on.'

'You rat!' Sue gasped.

'It's true!' he cried, his voice shaking in an inexplicable passion. 'She can't even stand up for her own flesh and blood!'

'Leave her alone!' Sue raged.

'I can't! She has to go! I have no intention of having a lodger around!' Cassian snapped.

With a whimper, Laura jerked her head away and found herself staring straight at the photo she'd taken of her son on his ninth birthday. Her heart lurched miserably.

Adam looked ecstatic. They'd spent the day at Skipton, where they'd explored the castle, picnicked by the river, and splashed out on a special treat of tea and cakes in a cosy café. Cheap and simple as day trips went, but a joy for both of them.

The recriminations surrounding his conception had been hard to bear. Yet, even in the depths of her shame, Laura had felt a growing joy. This child was hers. And when he was born, her emotions had overwhelmed her, unnerving her with their unexpected intensity.

Love had poured from her and it had felt as if her heart would burst with happiness. She'd never known she had such feelings. Her child had reached into her very core and found a well of passion hidden there.

For hours she had cuddled her baby, his warm, living flesh snuggling up to her. And it had been more than compensation for the hard, unremitting drudgery which Enid had imposed on her as a punishment for her 'lewd behaviour'.

She'd hardly cared because she had had her son to love. Someone to love her back.

Laura squared her shoulders. She would never let him down. Adam was horribly vulnerable and deeply sensitive. Cassian couldn't be allowed to uproot them both. Did he honestly imagine that they'd pack their bags without a murmur, and tramp the streets like vagabonds till someone took them in?

She flung up her head and spoke before she changed her mind. 'You're wrong about me! I *will* fight you for my home! Tooth and nail—'

'To defend your lion cub,' he murmured, his voice low and vibrating.

Her eyes hardened at his mockery. 'For the sake of my son,' she corrected in scathing tones, infuriated by his condescension. 'Sue, get going. I can deal with this better on my own. Besides, I'd rather you didn't witness the blood he sheds,' she muttered through her teeth.

'Sounds promising,' Cassian remarked lazily.

Laura ignored him because she thought she might choke with anger if she said anything. The situation clearly amused him. For her, it was deadly serious.

'Come on, Sue. Off you go and get those molars drilled,' she ordered tightly.

Secretly astonished by her own curt and decisive manner, she pushed her protesting friend towards the door.

Naturally, Sue resisted. 'I can't believe this! The worm turns! This I've gotta see!'

'I'll get the camera out,' Laura muttered. 'Please, please, go!'

'I want close-ups!' Sue hissed. 'A blow by blow account, when I get back!'

'Whatever! Go!'

It took her a minute or two before Sue could be budged but eventually she went, flinging dark and lurid warnings in Cassian's direction and promising Laura a stick of rock from Hong Kong to brain Cassian with if he was still around.

Quivering like a leaf, Laura shut the door, braced herself, and turned to face him. With Sue gone, it felt as if she was very alone. And she would be—till the following afternoon. Adam was going to his best friend's house after school and sleeping over. It was just her and Cassian, then.

Her heart thudded loudly in her chest at the strange pall of silence which seemed to have fallen on the house, intensifying the strained atmosphere.

Cassian was looking at her speculatively, his eyes half-closed in contemplation, a half-smile on his lips.

'It's a problem, isn't it?' he said mildly.

'The camera or the blood?' she flung back with rare sarcasm.

The black eyes twinkled disconcertingly. 'You and me. In this house together.'

The huskiness of his voice took her by surprise. It contrasted oddly with the intensity of his manner. There was a determined set to his jaw and the arch of his sensual mouth had flattened into a firm line.

'You can live anywhere. I can't—' she began.

'You must have friends who'd take you in,' he purred.

'I couldn't impose!'

'You don't have a choice.'

She felt close to tears of anger and frustration.

'You don't understand! I have to stay!' she insisted frantically.

'Why?'

'Because...' She went scarlet.

'Yes?' he prompted.

She stared at him, unwilling to expose her fear. But she saw no other way out.

Her eyes blazed with loathing. 'If you really want to know, I'm scared of going anywhere else!' she cried shakily.

He raised a sardonic eyebrow. 'Then it's time you did.'

She gasped. So much for compassion. But Cassian would never know what it was to be uncertain and shy, or to be uncomfortable in unfamiliar surroundings. Her pulses pounded as her heart rate accelerated.

'There's more,' she said, her lips dry with fear.

'Yes?'

She swallowed. This was deeply personal. Normally, wild horses wouldn't have dragged this out of her, but Cassian had to realise what this house meant to her.

'My...' She felt a fool. He was looking at her with cold hard eyes and she was having to expose her innermost secrets. For Adam, she told herself. And found the strength. Her eyes blazed blue and bright into his. 'My mother lived here,' she began tightly.

'So?'

She drew in a sharp breath of irritation. This wasn't going to get her anywhere. But...he'd adored his own mother. Wouldn't he understand?

'Cassian,' she grated. 'Is your mother still alive?'

He looked puzzled. 'Yes. Why?'

Thank heaven. Maybe she had a chance. 'You still see her, speak to her?'

'She's remarried. She lives in France, but yes, I see her.

And I speak to her each week. What are you getting at?'
he asked curiously.

She offered up a small prayer to the Fates. 'Imagine not
knowing anything about her. Not even how she looked.
Think what it would have been like, not to know that she's
beautiful, a gifted artist, and full of life and fire!' Her eyes
glowed feverishly with desperate passion.

'I don't see the—'

'Well, that's how it is for me!' she cried shakily. 'No
one will speak of my mother and all trace of her was removed the day she left.' Her voice broke and she took a
moment to steady herself. 'I wouldn't know anything at all
about her if it wasn't for Mr Walker—'

'Who?' he exclaimed sharply.

'He's someone in the village. A lonely old man with a
vile temper but he can't walk far so I do his weekly shopping. He gives me a list and money for what he needs. I
lug his shopping back, he complains about half of it and
we both feel better.'

Her eyes went dreamy for a moment. Out of the blue,
Mr Walker had once said that her mother was lovely. In
his opinion, he'd said, Diana had been wasted on boring
George Morris.

'What did he say about her?' Cassian asked warily.

She was surprised he was interested, but she smiled, remembering. 'That she was passionate about life.'

'Anything else?'

'Yes. He said she was kind and very beautiful.' Laura
sighed. 'Since I'm nothing like that, I think he was probably winding me up. When I asked him for more information he refused to say anything else.'

'I see,' he clipped, dark brows meeting hard together.

'The point is that this house means more to me than just
bricks and mortar and general sentimentality.' Desperate
now, she felt herself leaning forwards, punching out her

words. 'Thrushton Hall is all I have of my mother!' she jerked out miserably.

'Surely you must know about your mother—!'

'No! I don't!' Wouldn't he listen to her? Hadn't he heard? 'I don't know what she looked like, how or why she left me, *nothing*!'

She was aware of Cassian's stunned expression and took heart. He would see her plight and take pity on her.

'Cassian, other than the house, I have nothing else to remember her by, not one single item she ever possessed. Everything has vanished. The only actual trace of her is *me*!'

She steadied her voice, aware that it had been shaking so strongly with emotion that she'd been almost incoherent.

'I don't believe this!' he muttered.

'It's true!' she cried desperately. 'I've had to rely on my imagination! I've visualised her in this house, doing everyday things. That is where she must have stood to wash up, to cook,' she cried, pointing with a fierce jab of her finger. 'She must have sat at that very table to eat, to drink cups of tea. She would have stood at that window and gazed at the view of the soaring fells, just as I do. I can imagine her here and think of her going about her daily life. If—if I leave Thrushton,' she stumbled, 'I would have to leave behind those fragile half-memories of my mother. I'd have nothing at all left of her—and the little that I have is infinitely precious to me!' she sobbed.

She saw Cassian's jaw tighten and waited seemingly for an eternity before he answered.

'You must make enquiries about her,' he muttered, his tone flat and toneless.

Laura stared at him helplessly. How could she do that?

'I can't,' she retorted miserably.

'Afraid?' he probed, his eyes unusually watchful.

'Yes, if you must know!' she retorted with a baleful glare.

'Laura, you need to know—'

'I *can't*,' she cried helplessly. 'She's probably started a new life somewhere and I could ruin it by turning up on her doorstep. I couldn't do that to her. If it was all right for us to meet, she would have come to see me. I can't take the initiative, can I?'

He was silent, his face stony. But she knew what he was thinking. That perhaps her mother hadn't wanted to be reminded of her 'mistake'.

Closing her mind to such a horrible idea, she lifted her chin in an attempt to appear tough. Though even a fool would have noticed her stupid, feeble trembling.

'You must learn the truth—' he began huskily.

'No!'

She wrung her hands, frustrated that he couldn't see how scared she was of confronting her mother. Maybe she was flighty. Maybe she'd had a string of lovers. Maybe...

'Cassian,' she croaked, voicing her worst fear, 'I can't pursue this. I—I just couldn't face being rejected by her.'

'I don't think—'

'How the devil do you know!' she yelled. 'She left me, didn't she? Though...I suppose she knew that George would have won custody, whatever she did. She'd run away. He'd been looking after me and was a lawyer, after all. Mother must have known she didn't have a chance. To be honest, I don't even know if there was a court hearing about me. There might have been—and she might have tried to take me with her. I'll never know. Nobody would ever talk about her.' Slowly her head lifted till her troubled eyes met Cassian's. 'Mr Walker said she was full of life. Knowing how *your* mother felt, I understand why anyone with fire and energy would have found it difficult to live here,' she said with dignity.

Cassian looked uncomfortable. 'Laura,' he said in a gravelly voice, 'this is nothing to do with me. Not one of your arguments is sufficient reason for you to stay. Excuse me.'

He strode into the hall. She heard the sound of men moving about, presumably bringing in his possessions. She buried her head in her hands. She'd failed.

Cassian saw her emerging from the kitchen a few moments later, her eyes pink from crying, silver tear-track streaks glistening on her face. He gritted his teeth and continued to organise the stacking of his few belongings in the spacious hall.

Behind his bent back, he could hear the fast rasp of her breathing and sensed she was close to hysteria. And he felt as if he'd whipped a puppy.

'All done, guv,' announced one of the men.

Grateful for the diversion, he gave Len and Charlie his undivided attention. 'Thanks. Great meeting you,' he said warmly, shaking the men's hands in turn.

He slid his wallet from his back pocket and handed over the fee plus a tip, brushing away their astonished refusals of such a large sum of money. What was cash to him? It came easily and went the same way.

Charlie had told him about his new baby and Len was nearing retirement. They could both do with a little extra and he believed passionately in circulating money while he had the earning power.

'I had a windfall. Might as well share it, eh?' he explained. Like an obscene advance from a film company.

'Yeah? You're a gent,' said Len in awe.

'Thanks,' added Charlie, looking stunned.

'Have a pint on me.'

Len grinned. 'Treat the wife to a slap-up meal and a holiday, more like!'

'Buy a baby buggy!' enthused Charlie.

He saw them out, found them shaking his hand again and accepted an invitation to visit Charlie's baby and to have tea and cakes with Len and his wife. After much scribbling of addresses, he returned to the tense and angry Laura.

'What are you trying to do by gossiping out there—drive me to screaming pitch?!' she demanded furiously, her hands on shapely hips.

He stole a moment to admire them. 'Being friendly. Would you prefer I dismissed them with a curt nod and a growl?' he enquired.

She flushed. 'No...oh, you're *impossible*!'

He felt pleased. Her eyes were sparkling, a hot flush brightening her cheeks. If only he could release her emotions...

He bit back an impulse to invite her to stay so he could do just that, and followed up her remark instead.

'I just live by a different code from you. Now...will I push you into suicide mode if I just check I've got all my possessions here?'

She blinked her huge eyes, dark lashes fluttering as she eyed the stack of boxes, his luggage, and three bags of shopping.

'Do you mean...that this is all you own in the whole world?'

'It's all I need. Books, computer stuff and a few mementoes. Plus a few changes of clothes and some food stores.'

'I don't understand you,' she muttered.

'Not many people do. Now, this is what I've decided,' he said brusquely, suddenly needing to get away from the censure of her accusing eyes. 'I'd booked a room in a hotel in Grassington because I didn't know what state the house would be in. I'll go there now and leave you to start looking for temporary accommodation. Someone will take you in for a few days till you can find somewhere permanent. I'll be back in the morning. To take possession.'

He turned on his heel. Flinched at her horrified intake of breath as it rasped through emotion-choked airways.

'Cassian!' she pleaded in desperation.

But he'd opened the door, was striding up the path and

ignoring the sound of her weeping. It would be good for her, he kept telling himself, wrenching at the door handle of his car.

She needed to find out the truth about her mother. But first she'd have to stand up for herself, to gain some strength of will—and being forced to move would make her take her life in her hands at last.

He crunched the gears. And accelerated away, angry with her for making him feel such a swine.

CHAPTER THREE

WHEN he turned up the next morning she was beating the hell out of a lump of dough and he couldn't help smiling because her small fists were clearly using it as a substitute for his head.

Her glare would have put off a seasoned terrorist but, knowing how normally reclusive she was, he could only be pleased. This was precisely the reaction he'd hoped for.

'Any progress?' he asked, coming straight to the point.

'No.' She jammed her teeth together and kneaded the bread with a fascinating ferocity. 'If you must know, I didn't try! And if you're looking for coffee,' she said, as he opened and shut cupboards at random, 'you're out of luck. There isn't any.'

He went to find some in the supplies he'd brought, came back and put on the kettle. The bread dough looked so elastic she could have used it for bungy jumping.

'You did discuss leaving with your son, didn't you?' he enquired.

Laura slammed the dough into a bowl and covered it with a cloth. 'You didn't give me a chance to tell you,' she said grimly, pushing the bowl into the warming oven to prove and slamming the heavy iron door with some force. 'Adam's been with a friend. I won't see him till this afternoon after school. Besides…' Her face crumpled and he realised that she looked very tired and pale as if she'd been up most of the night. 'I can't tell him!' she confessed helplessly.

'You can. You're stronger than you think—' he began.

'But *he's* not!'

Quite frantic now, she began to fling fresh ingredients

into a mixing bowl and he began to think that the resulting cake would weigh a ton.

'In what way isn't he strong?' he asked quietly.

'Every way,' she muttered, measuring out flour carelessly. 'Cassian, *you* know what it's like to be uprooted from somewhere familiar. You loved the narrow boat where you lived with your mother before you came here after her marriage, and you loathed Thrushton—'

'Not the house itself, or the countryside,' he corrected, wondering what she'd say if he brushed away the dusting of flour on her nose and cheeks. It made her look cute and appealing and he didn't want that. It was very distracting. 'Just the atmosphere. The stifling rules,' he said, miraculously keeping track of the conversation.

'Well, moving is traumatic, especially when you're a child. Can't you put yourself in Adam's place and see how awful it would be for him to leave the place of his birth?' she implored, pushing away her hair with the back of her hand. 'Making friends is hard for him. He'd find it a nightmare settling into another school.'

'Life's tough. Children need to be challenged,' he said softly. He passed her a coffee.

'Challenged?!' She flung in the flour haphazardly and began to fold it into the cake mixture as if declaring war on it. 'He's sensitive. It would destroy him!' she cried, her face aflame with desperation.

'Here. That'll turn into a rugby ball if you're not careful. Let me.'

He took the bowl from her shaking hands, combined the flour and the abused mixture with a metal spoon then scooped it all into a cake tin. Gently he slid the tin into the baking oven and checked the clock.

She stood in helpless misery, her hands constantly twisting together.

'Thanks,' she mumbled.

'You say your son is sensitive,' he mused. 'Is he happy where he is at school now?'

She frowned. 'N-no—'

'Well, then!'

'But another one could be worse—!'

'Or better.'

'I doubt it. He'd be such a bag of nerves that he'd turn up on his first day with ''victim'' written all over his face,' she wailed. Her eyes were haunted. 'You can't do this to my child! I love him! He's everything I have!'

His guts twisted and he had to wait before he could speak.

'And you? How will you feel, living elsewhere?'

His voice had suddenly softened, caressing her gently. She drew in a sharp breath and shuddered with horror.

'I can't bear to think of going,' she mumbled pitifully. 'I love every inch of this house. I know it, and the garden, the village, the hills and the dales, as well as I know the back of my hand. There's no lovelier place on God's earth. My heart is here. Tear me away,' she said, her voice shaking with passion, 'and you rip out a part of me!'

'I'm sorry that you will both find it hard,' he said curtly. 'But…there it is. That's life. One door closes, another one opens.'

Laura gasped at his callousness. It was as she feared. He was determined on his course of action. She turned away as tears rushed up, choking her. Her hands gripped the back of a chair for support as she imagined Adam facing a new playground, new teachers, new, more intimidating bullies…

'All right, Cassian!' She whirled back in a fury. 'You open and close all the doors you want—I'm staying put!'

He smiled faintly and his slow and thorough gaze swept her from head to toe.

'Flour on your face,' he murmured.

Before she knew it, his fingers were lightly travelling over her skin while she gazed into his lazily smiling eyes,

eyes so dark and liquid that she felt she was melting into a warm Mediterranean sea.

By accident, his caressing fingers touched her mouth. And instantly something seared through her like a heated lance, tightening every nerve she possessed and sending an electric charge into her system.

She struggled to focus, to forget the terrible effect he was having on her. He was throwing her out. Going gooey-eyed wouldn't help her at *all*. Rot him—was he doing this deliberately? Her eyes blazed with anger.

'If you want me to go, you'll have to get the removal men to carry me out!' she flung wildly.

'No need. I'd carry you out myself. I don't think it would be beyond my capabilities,' he mused.

In a split second she saw herself in his arms, helpless, at his mercy…'Touch me and you'll regret it!' she spat, thoroughly uncomfortable with her treacherous feelings.

'Yes,' he agreed slowly, apparently fascinated by her parted lips and her accelerated breathing. 'I think I might.' Equally slowly, a dazzling grin spread across his face. It was at once wicked and beguiling and made Laura's stomach contract. 'But,' he drawled, 'that wouldn't stop me from doing so.'

She blinked in confusion. There were undercurrents here she didn't understand. Somehow she broke the spell that had kept her eyes locked to his and she looked around desperately for a diversion.

'I'd fight you!' she muttered.

'Mmm. Then I'd have to hold you very, very tightly, wouldn't I?' he purred.

Her throat dried. Almost without realising, she began to tidy the dresser, despite the fact she was so agitated that she kept knocking things over.

Cassian came up behind her. Although there had been no sound, she knew he was near because the hairs on the back of her neck stood on end and her spine tingled. Sure enough, his hand reached out, covering hers where it rested on a figurine she'd toppled.

'You'll break something,' he chided, his breath whispering warm and soft over her ear, like a summer breeze in the valley.

'I don't give a toss!' she jerked out stupidly, snatching her hand away.

He caught the flying figure deftly and set it on the dresser. His arm was whipcord strong, his hands big but with surprisingly long, delicate fingers.

'Laura, surrender. You can't fight the inevitable.'

She blinked, her huge eyes fixed on his neatly manicured nails. Her body was in turmoil and she didn't know why. It was her head that ought to be in frantic disarray.

She should be panicking about her eviction. Instead, she was finding herself totally transfixed by his breathing, the cottony smell of his T-shirt, the accompanying warm maleness...

Oh, help me, someone! she groaned inwardly, trying to gather her wits.

'It can't be inevitable! Have pity on us!' she whispered.

'I am. That's why I'm chucking you out. And when I do, would you like a fireman's lift, or something more conventional?' he murmured in amusement, turning her to face him.

Laura's knees weren't functioning properly. She wobbled and he steadied her. He was incredibly close, his smooth, tanned face sympathetic and kind. It didn't make sense. But his gentle smile broke her resistance. For a terrible, shaming instant, she was horribly tempted to reach up and kiss that inviting mouth so that the tingling of her own lips could be assuaged.

Her eyes widened at her temerity. This was madness! Where were her inhibitions when she needed them? She'd never felt like this. Never had such an overwhelming urge

to abandon what was decent and proper and to submit to
physical temptations!

It was a relief that he couldn't know how she felt. The
unguarded, unwanted and definitely unhinged response of
her own body shocked her. It felt as if she was glowing.
Erotic sensations were centred in places where he shouldn't
have reached. It was awful. Like finding she enjoyed sin.

Shame brought high colour to her cheeks. A terrible
thought flashed through her mind. Perhaps she was a slut.
Perhaps her mother had been… *No!* Her hand flew to her
mouth in horror, dismayed where his casual behaviour had
taken her.

'Laura,' he murmured, drawing her imperceptibly closer.

'Let me go! I told you!' she moaned, wriggling away
from the pressure of his hands and emerging hot and flustered because of the skin-tingling way they had slid down
her arms. She moved back warily. 'I don't want you to
touch me!' she stormed. 'Let's get this straight! If you do
force me out, I'll come straight back in!'

His eyes danced with bright amusement. 'I'd lock the
door.'

'I'd break a window!' she retorted heatedly.

'Do you intend your son to use the same point of entry?'

Laura ground her teeth in frustration. Her argument was
futile and they both knew it. That didn't help her temper
much.

'So you turn out a woman and a child, both of whom
were born in this house! How do you think you'll be treated
by people in this village?' she flared.

'Like a leper. However, it's not something that would
disturb my sleep,' he replied gravely.

No. It wouldn't. Cassian never worried about the opin-
ions of others. In her desperation she tried another tack. A
last-ditch attempt to find a scrap of compassion in Cassian's
granite heart.

'Adam is asthmatic. Emotional upsets can bring on an

attack. Do you want his health on your conscience?' she demanded.

'That would be unpleasant for all of us,' he admitted. 'What do you suggest we do?'

Her mouth fell open. 'What?'

Quite calmly, Cassian perched on the kitchen table, one long leg swinging freely and his steady gaze pinning Laura to the spot.

'I've bought the house. I want to live in it. So do you. That suggests a conflict of interests. How do you propose we deal with the situation?'

She was astonished. She hadn't expected negotiating tactics.

'Tell Tony you've made a mistake! Get him to buy it back!' she pleaded.

Cassian shook his head. 'No use. He'll have paid off his debtors to save himself from being beaten up again.'

'Again?! What do you mean?' She felt the colour drain from her face. 'Where is he? What's happened to him?' she asked in agitation.

'You're surprisingly concerned, considering Tony's indifference to you,' he observed. 'If I recall, he was the favoured child. He went from public school to university, whereas you were destined to leave school early. It never bothered him that your lives were unequal. You didn't figure in his life at all.'

'There was a crucial difference between Tony and me,' she pointed out sharply.

'Sure,' Cassian scathed. 'He was a selfish jerk. You were a doormat—'

'I—I was…!' OK. She was a doormat. He didn't have to say so! 'I was hardly in a position to demand my rights,' she said stiltedly. 'I had no blood ties with anyone in this house and you know that. It's hardly surprising he had all the advantages. I was lucky—'

'*Lucky?*' he barked, leaping to his feet angrily.

'Yes! They brought me up. I was fed and clothed—'

'You were crushed,' he snapped. His eyes blazed down at her, sapping her strength with their ferocity. 'And you're *grateful* because they offered you the basic human needs! Laura, they systematically browbeat you. They punished you for what your mother did to the oh-so-important George Morris, solicitor of this parish. They turned you into an obedient, colourless, cowering mouse, afraid of opening your mouth in case you said the wrong thing—!'

'Don't you criticise my family!' she cried hotly. 'It's none of your business how we lived! I don't care what you think of me…!'

She gulped. Because she did care. It upset her that he saw her as such a wimp. An obedient, colourless, cowering mouse! That was an awful description. Was she that pathetic?

Muddled, she stood there, her chest heaving, wondering why he was so angry and why she kept losing the composure which had always been such an integral part of her.

That was because he'd flung her into her worst nightmare. He was knocking away all her props. Leaving her with nothing. Perhaps she could plead with Tony herself…

'Tony,' she reminded him, her voice thin with panic. She sat down, shaking. 'Just tell me what's happened to him!'

Cassian felt like shaking her. She still saw justification in the way she'd been treated as a child. And yet cracks were beginning to appear in her armour. Rebellion simmered inside that tense body. She might have been taught to abhor passion but it was there, nevertheless and the thought excited him more than it should.

Inexplicably he'd wanted to press his lips on her pink, pouting mouth and her unavailability had only made the urge stronger. He couldn't understand his reaction. He'd been celibate for a long time and many women had tried to steer him from his chosen path, using all the tricks in the book and then some.

Tricks he could deflect. This was something else. Whether he liked it or not, Laura was reaching something deeper in him without even knowing what she was doing.

Curbing his rampaging instincts, he set about hurrying her departure before her temptations proved his undoing. Women could be dynamite at the best of times. He dare not get tangled up with someone like Laura. That would be dangerous in the extreme for both of them.

Pity, he found himself musing recklessly. It was such a luscious, kissable mouth... And he hungered for it more than was wise.

Grimly Cassian subdued his lurching passions. He could be hard on himself when necessary. And this was essential.

'I met Tony in Marrakesh—' he began at a gallop.

'*Marrakesh!*' she exclaimed, as if it were the planet Mars.

He gave a faint smile. To her, it probably was.

'Stupidly he'd swindled some thugs and they'd beaten him up. I got out the sticking plasters, let him stay for a while—'

'You have a house in Marrakesh?' she asked, wide-eyed.

Cassian perched on the table again. 'No, I rented rooms. Tony hotbedded with Fee, a stripper, who I—'

'*What?*' Her eyes were even wider, her mouth now joining in the amazement. She was wonderfully transparent. 'You...lived with a...stripper?!'

'Two, actually.' Before her jaw dropped any further and she did herself an injury, he added, 'We weren't cohabiting, I hasten to add. Same house, different rooms. Loads of space, no obligations to one another, come and go as you like...a perfect arrangement. No commitment, company when you want it, solitude when you don't.'

'But...strippers?'

Disapproval came from every line of her body. He decided she needed to have her judgement shaken up.

'Don't let the job fool you. Fee's a sweetie, with a very

strict moral code. Comes from Islington. You'd like her. Runs a shelter for sick animals in her spare time.'

'You're kidding me!' she scoffed.

'No, word of honour. It's partly why she let Tony stay. She has a warm heart.'

'I bet. So…what does…''hot-bedded'' mean, then?!' she asked warily.

He couldn't help but smile again, seeing that he was stretching her knowledge of the world a little too fast, a little too far.

'It's not as interesting as it sounds. The strippers worked at night so Tony had the use of Fee's bed in their room. During the day they slept, and he mooched about on the roof. It's flat. A kind of garden,' he explained.

'Warm-hearted or not, I don't see why they'd let a stranger invade their privacy.'

'It was a favour to me.'

'Oh?'

It was a very meaningful and glacial Aunt Enid kind of 'oh', but he wasn't going to explain how he'd got the girls out of trouble with the police, who'd been harassing them in the hope of some 'action'.

'Anyway,' he said, 'I suggested an answer to his cash flow problem. He was relieved to sell up. I got the impression he felt nothing for the Dales.'

'No, he didn't,' Laura admitted.

'Last I heard, he was planning his escape to Gibraltar with what was left of the cash.' He glanced at her sharply. 'How soon can you go?'

She bit her lip. 'You're heartless!' she flung.

He grunted. 'Practical. I'm not good at living cheek-by-jowl with other people.'

'I remember,' she said caustically and he gave a lop-sided grin. 'Cassian…' She paused, then seemed to pluck up courage. 'Let me explain the difficulty of my situation.'

He frowned. 'You've done that already, at extraordinary length.'

'Please! Give me a chance!'

Her huge blue eyes transfixed him. He saw that she was close to tears and felt a pang of sympathy. Even though her plight had shaken him more than he would have liked, he could cope with this. He'd handled any number of awkward situations in his life.

'All right. I'll listen—briefly. But, I warn you, I won't change my mind.'

'Do you blame me for trying?' she asked, her face wan.

'Go on, then. Make your pitch if you think it's worth fighting for. Tooth and nail, I think you said. And Sue will expect to see blood on the floor when she next calls in,' he mocked, deliberately goading her.

Rebellion flared in her eyes and brought a new strength to her trembling mouth.

'She's going to Hong Kong for two weeks. It'll have dried by then,' she said tartly.

Cassian laughed. 'Well give it a go,' he encouraged, eyes crinkling in amusement.

She took a moment to compose herself, knowing that she must be calm. Adam's future depended on what she said and how she said it. This time, she must let Cassian know her son's needs.

'I want to tell you about Adam in a little more detail,' she said gently. 'The kind of person he is. Why I'm so anxious about him.'

Cassian marvelled at the change that came over her. The expression on her face had became suffused with tenderness and he felt his heart soften. She could love, he thought, his pulses quickening.

'Yes?' he snapped.

His curtness had no impact on her at all. She was totally absorbed in thinking of her beloved son. That's pure love, he mused. And marvelled at the luminous quality of her eyes.

'He was born prematurely. I think now,' she said softly, 'that when I was pregnant I did too much physical work around the house for too long.'

'Sounds like Enid. Perhaps she wanted you to lose your baby,' he muttered.

She winced. 'Perhaps. I can't deny that's a possibility. She made it clear that my pregnancy was all the more reason for me to pull my weight. Anyway, he was a sickly baby and cried a lot. I found myself protecting him, watching out for the slightest indication that he might be starting another chest infection. And then, one day, he—oh, Cassian, it was so awful!' she whispered.

'Tell me,' he said softly.

His heart went out to her. She'd been treated very badly. Someone ought to give her a good time, make her happy...

'He had his first asthma attack. I thought he was dying! He was rushed into hospital and put in an oxygen tent. I knew then that he was more important to me than life itself. From that moment on, I've had to watch his health very carefully,' she said, her voice low and so tender that he almost envied the child. 'It's important that he's not stressed. If he's badly upset then he gets an asthma attack. I've had to work around them, of course. It's what mothers do.'

He grunted. 'Work at what?'

'I did a computer course,' she replied. 'I did well, had a natural aptitude, but I had to abandon it. Adam was ill so often that I couldn't take on anything full-time or permanent because I had to look after him.'

'Tough,' he conceded, his eyes narrowed as he studied her.

She showed no signs of resentment that her son's health had imprisoned her in a financial straitjacket. Pure love shone from her eyes. He wondered idly what it would be like to win the heart of a woman with such deep, hidden passions.

Frightening, he decided. She'd expect total togetherness. His idea of hell.

'It's not tough,' she said, her expression tender. 'He's so uncomplaining and I...like being with him,' she added more briskly, as if reluctant to express affection for her son.

'How did you survive? Social Services?' he hazarded.

'No!' She looked shocked. 'I worked for ages as a waitress in a Grassington hotel but the new owner has daughters who can do my job.' She put on a bright smile. 'They're gorgeous blondes with big bosoms,' she explained with a laugh of self-deprecation.

He tried to stop himself, but he found his glance flicking down and the way she was hugging herself revealed more than she knew, the shirt pulling tightly over firm, high breasts, lusher than he could have imagined.

He felt heat suffuse him and frowned with annoyance. He'd seen breasts before. He wasn't a curious teenager any more.

'Pulls in the trade, you must admit,' he said shortly.

'Oh, I can't blame him for employing his family, or anyone who's really attractive,' she said without rancour. 'I have no illusions about myself.'

You should look in the damn mirror! he thought sourly in the pause that followed. How could she miss what he could see? And yet he dared not tell her. For a start, she'd never believe him—and he didn't have time to convince her. Nor would it be in his interests.

'And, as you have already said, you're out of work again,' he said flatly.

'With a sickly child,' she emphasised.

She crossed and neatly arranged her eye-catching legs. Her face lifted to his earnestly. Cassian hardened his heart. The welfare state would provide.

'So?'

'I can't just walk out and rent somewhere. I have no savings. But I am actively searching for a job and when I get it, I'll pay *you* rent. You don't want this house. You can't want it. You bought it out of the goodness of your heart, to get Tony out of a hole—'

'Huh! If he were in a hole, I'd hire an excavator to make it deeper,' he drawled, moved by her situation despite himself. Yet common sense argued that it was still in her best interests to leave. 'I'm not charitable where he's concerned. I'm here because I want to be.'

'But—!'

'No buts. This has gone on long enough. I'll make it easy for you, Laura. A compromise. Pack your stuff. When your son comes home I'll drive you both to a hotel of your choice and I'll pay for you to stay there till you find a job. Can't say fairer than that.'

He leaned back, pleased with his generous solution. Laura looked defeated. For some reason that didn't give him the satisfaction he'd expected.

The muscles in her heart-wrenchingly sweet face tightened as she struggled not to cry and he had a wild moment when he almost moved forwards to take her in his arms and soothe her panic with promises he couldn't keep.

The tears defied her, trickling from the corners of her eyes. Cassian gritted his teeth to stop himself from backtracking.

'I couldn't let you pay our hotel bill!' she croaked shakily.

'I couldn't do otherwise,' he found himself saying.

'I have my pride.'

'So has the entire population of Yorkshire.'

'It's your revenge, isn't it?' she mumbled.

Cassian frowned. 'What for?'

She hung her head. 'For what Enid and my f-father did to you,' she sniffed.

He was appalled. 'No! I—'

'Then *why?*' she wailed.

'That's my business. I want you to go. Don't you see that—'

She wasn't listening. Her head was angled in an attitude of listening. He heard the sound of feet: someone running—stumbling—up the path.

'It's Adam! Something's wrong!' she jerked out, with a mother's inexplicable certainty.

Hastily she rubbed her tear-stained face with her fists then jumped up and flung open the door. Past her rigidly held body, he saw a mud-splattered boy with dishevelled blond hair and a panic-stricken expression come skidding to a halt outside.

'Adam!' she whispered.

Cassian frowned and rose to his feet. The child was obviously in distress, and by the looks of him he'd been in a fight, but neither he nor his mother were making any move towards one another.

They both stood as if frozen to the ground, staring in consternation, some kind of signal going between them that prevented them from physical contact.

A chill went down his spine. Enid's tongue had removed something more crucial than defiance from Laura. It had killed Laura's ability to show love.

'I—I fell over!' Adam claimed, trying to be brave. But his mouth was all over the place.

'Oh, Adam…!' Laura was evidently distressed. Her hands hovered in front of her as if she was desperate to cuddle her son but had been forbidden to do so. 'I—you…! You—you should be at school—'

Cassian could bear no more. He pushed Laura aside and placed a firm arm around the quivering child's shoulders.

'Cup of tea, I think,' he declared cheerfully, easing him through the door. 'Then a scrub down with the yard brush and a bit of TLC for those bruises. Falling over's quite a shock, isn't it?' he chattered, getting the shaken child into a comfortable armchair in the kitchen and crouching down beside him. 'I did it a lot as a child.' He grinned. 'I seemed to get in the way of other boys' feet.'

He tensed when Laura's hand came past his ear and brushed the hair back from her son's forehead to reveal the bruise which Cassian had already spotted. He was an expert on bruises. And bullying. Particularly from adults.

'Poor Adam!' Laura leaned forwards and hesitantly kissed the purple bruise and then briefly touched her son's hot face. 'I'll put the kettle on,' she said huskily, as if overcome.

'Thanks, Mum.'

Adam bent to untie his shoe laces and Cassian knew he was trying to hide his tears. To be strong. To cultivate a stiff upper lip. Anything to stop real emotion from emerging. Emotion was a bad word at Thrushton Hall.

He could hear George Morris's voice now, echoing down the years.

'Stop crying!' Morris would beg the temperamental Bathsheba in horror. Or…'Don't laugh so loud!…' 'Don't dance like that—it's…unseemly, you're a married woman!…' Or maybe 'Calm yourself!…Don't yell…'

Ridiculous. The man had married his mother because he'd adored her exuberance. And then had set about curbing it so that she fitted in with the silent and repressed household over which he'd presided.

It wasn't surprising that the deeply repressed Laura was afraid of expressing her real feelings.

Cassian found the situation interesting. There seemed to be a kind of agreement between Laura and her child. A tacit acceptance, perhaps, that there should be the minimum of affection displayed, one or two small gestures sufficing for deep concern.

Intriguingly, she had put her hand on the arm of the chair where Adam was sitting. Cassian had noticed that Adam had imperceptibly leaned in that direction so that his body was inches from his mother's restless fingers.

He couldn't believe what was happening. This was a kind of distant comfort, practised by two people who didn't dare to let go in case they betrayed their emotions.

The situation struck deep at his heart and he was moved more than he would have liked. Wordlessly, hampered by no inhibitions, he reached out to hug the shaking child and to let him know what human warmth could be like. He rubbed the thin, bony back in sympathy.

'Let's get your muddy shoes and jumper off, shall we?' he suggested gently.

As the child complied with a worrying submissiveness, Cassian reflected that the relationship between Laura and Adam couldn't be more different than the closeness between him and Jai. Laura would be shocked if she ever saw their mutual expressions of love. He and his son had no problems about expressing their emotions.

A surge of longing careered unhindered through him. He wanted his child near him. Missed him like hell. In a reflex action, he clutched Adam more tightly.

'Who...are you?' Adam asked timidly.

He smiled down mistily. 'Cassian.'

The trembling stopped. Tears were knuckled away in a gesture that mimicked Laura's.

'Gosh! I've heard of you!'

He grimaced. 'Don't tell me!' he said, pretending to groan. 'I was surly and rude and ignored your mother while I was here!'

Adam shook his head, his blue Laura-eyes bright with eagerness.

'I dunno about that. But Mum said you knew every plant and insect and bird and you could find your way around the countryside blindfold!'

Cassian glanced at Laura in amusement. 'Your mother is very kind to concentrate on my few good points.'

'Cassian's come to stay,' Laura said, putting a mug of tea by Adam's elbow. Her eyes challenged Cassian to say anything further.

'Oh, gosh, cool!' enthused Adam.

Cassian frowned at Laura. He'd deal with her later. He fixed Adam with a sober but friendly gaze.

'So. Spill the beans,' he said quietly. 'What happened?'

'I—' Adam faltered, clearly unable to look into Cassian's steady eyes and tell a lie. There was a long pause. It was the silence before a confession and Cassian waited patiently for the child to begin. 'Well…at break-time they said my Mum was a stupid feeble wimp, like me, and—and that we're silly drips with marshmallow instead of guts!' he said with a huge, indignant sniff.

There was another pause. Cassian prayed that Laura wouldn't react or speak. The boy needed a silence to fill with words. Any interruption might make the kiddie clam up. To his utter relief, Laura didn't even move and after fiddling with his fingers for a while, Adam began again.

'I t-tried to ignore them, like Mum said, but they pushed me into the nettles then jumped on m-me and pinched my packed lunch!'

Tears rolled down his cheeks again and Cassian felt his heart aching for the distressed child.

'Here,' he said huskily, grasping Adam's hands strongly in his.

'Oh, my darling!' Laura sobbed.

And to Cassian's surprise, she pushed him aside and drew her son into an awkward embrace. She was crying too, utter misery on her face.

Cassian rose, made two more mugs of tea and took the cake out of the oven. It pained him to see Laura rocking her child and trying to control her weeping.

They needed love and support. Someone to give them confidence. Bullying made him feel sick. Even the thought of it disrupted his laid-back approach to life and made him irrational, his emotions churning chaotically as anger, resentment, pity and past terrors filled his head.

He'd been secretly bullied by George Morris. Taunted, spat upon, and beaten by older kids at senior school. The sheer helplessness had made him seethe with rage and frustration.

And he was seething now, hurting for Adam's sake, loathing those who attacked anyone who didn't conform to some imaginary 'norm'.

He couldn't bear it. He wanted to crack heads together, yell, terrify...anything so that Laura and her child would never weep like this again. He wanted to hug them both, tell them he'd deal with the problem, see their tears dry up and their faces turn to him trustingly. To see them smile.

He found himself shaking—whether from passion or fear at where his thoughts were leading, he wasn't sure.

At that moment, he knew that he couldn't turn them out—not yet, anyway. And the cold certainty iced his spine with apprehension.

He was walking into dangerous quicksand. He loathed living with other people. Found their pettiness and knee-jerk rules irritating. Yet the urge to offer a temporary respite for Laura and Adam was so overwhelming that it couldn't be denied. It seemed he cared about them.

He drew in a sharp breath. For a man who needed to be free that was extremely worrying.

CHAPTER FOUR

LAURA crossly banged pans about as she prepared a scrap lunch. How Cassian had persuaded Adam to go up for a bath without protest—and got him giggling as well in the process—she'd never know.

But before she could think straight, Adam had come hurrying back downstairs in a holey old jumper and faded jeans, his face pink and shiny with eagerness as if something exciting awaited.

She supposed it did. Cassian.

Now Adam sat in smiling assent while Cassian gently and expertly smoothed the cuts and bruises with some cream he'd dug from his First Aid kit.

Adam had spurned her usual stuff, beguiled by the promise that Cassian's remedy was herbal and 'brilliant, I use it all the time when I fall off mountains and things'.

Huh! What was she suddenly? Redundant? The mince suffered a fierce pounding with the spoon. Cassian had made her look both callous and, now, hopelessly inadequate.

When she'd seen Adam struggling desperately to be brave, she hadn't known what to do. Should she respect his attempt or give in to her maternal instinct and comfort him?

It had always been an unwritten rule between them that Adam should try to overcome the bullying on his own. He'd made that clear the first time she'd indignantly tried to interfere on his behalf.

But now Cassian had changed the rule. And, even more infuriating, his tactics of firmness, humour and sympathy had worked, defusing Adam's shock and making him feel better about himself.

With vicious strokes, she grated some cheese and put it aside then flung carrots, onions and turnips into the mince to make it go further.

Adam ought to be sitting with his shoulders hunched, chest heaving, clinging for dear life to his asthma inhaler. That's what invariably happened after something like this.

Instead, he was laughing at some improbable tale Cassian was relating about walking in the foothills of the Himalayas—Him*arlee*as he pretentiously called them— when he'd slid over fifty feet down a slope and ended up in a particularly magnificent heap of yak manure. Huh! As if!

'We ought to let the school know you're here, Adam,' she said shortly, interrupting Cassian's fairy stories.

'Phone them after lunch,' Cassian suggested with a languid stretch.

'We don't have a phone.' Crossly she met his astonished eyes. 'Too expensive. I'll have to go to the school—'

'That's ridiculous!' he protested. 'It's a four-mile round trip. Take off that hair shirt. You can use my mobile or take my car.'

'I'll phone. Thank you,' she muttered.

'Mum can't drive,' explained Adam.

'Perhaps I should teach her,' Cassian growled.

There was a sudden silence. She looked at Cassian, startled and flustered by his remark. Though he looked more than a little startled too. Her heart thudded. Surely this meant she had a reprieve! Long enough for her to learn to drive!

Adam looked impressed. She knew he dearly wanted her to join the human race and acquire a driving licence. But what was the point if she couldn't afford to own a car? Yet that didn't matter. The reprieve did.

'You won't tell them what happened, will you, Mum?' Adam asked anxiously.

'I can't have you being hurt like this—' she began fretfully.

'Please!' he begged, looking petrified. 'You'll make it worse!'

She looked at him helplessly. What did you do? What was right, in the long run? Did she make her son a total outcast by complaining, or was he to be battered on a regular basis?

Extraordinarily, she found herself searching out Cassian, wondering if he had an answer to the problem. She quivered. There was a melting tenderness in his eyes and it confused her.

'*You* were bullied,' she said to him in a low tone, remembering the torn clothes, and the cuts and bruises he'd often be sporting. He'd always told Aunt Enid that he'd been in a fight, but had never asked for help. And suddenly the bullying had stopped. 'What do *you* think?'

'I didn't want adult interference,' he said quietly. 'But that's because I wanted to find my own way of dealing with the bullying. There isn't one solution. Each person has a different need. Some don't have the resources to cope alone. Adam, if you think you can change from being a victim to a winner, then go for it.'

He was wise, she thought, seeing her son straighten as if he was growing in stature. Suddenly she saw that Cassian could help Adam so much. A tremor took her unawares, making her lips part at the thought of Cassian here, taking a part in their daily lives.

'How long are you staying?' Adam asked him.

She winced at the wistful note. Her son was revelling in male company. Suddenly she felt isolated.

'A while. Moving in tonight,' came the easy reply. It was coupled with a dazzling smile.

'Cool!'

She shot a glance at Cassian and found that he was regarding her wryly. The odd sensations crept into her loins again. They were like small spasms, tugging and relaxing.

Quite unnervingly enjoyable. She bit her lip and clenched all her muscles hard.

'...yes, I was twelve when I first came to Thrushton,' Cassian was saying.

'Did you like it here?' Adam asked eagerly.

'Hated Aunt Enid, loved Thrushton,' Cassian replied with blistering honesty.

Adam giggled. 'Why?'

'I regret to say that Enid was a cow. A strict and humourless woman who thought children should be neither seen nor heard. I think she would have preferred them to have sprung from the womb as fully trained adults with a degree in silence and obedience.'

'Cassian!' Laura reproved, while Adam gazed in delighted shock.

'I can hear her voice now,' he said, looking pointedly at her and Laura blushed in bitter recognition because she'd caught herself reproving Adam's small and rare misdemeanours with Enid's sharp little voice. Cassian had the bit between his teeth and was galloping on. 'Her favourite word was "don't",' he said blithely. 'And her tongue had been dipped in snake venom. She had a way of gnashing her teeth that makes me think now that she could have crushed Terminator I, II and III in her jaws.'

Adam laughed, awe-struck by Cassian's frankness. 'But you liked Thrushton,' he said, pleased.

'Oh, yes. Out there...' He paused. Laura gulped, her senses beguiled. His face had become soft, quite beautiful in its dreaminess. 'It's wild and free and open. Magnificent scenery. Takes you at once from your small, inward world and places your life in a greater context. Don't you think?'

Laura was stunned to learn how he'd felt. That was why he'd spent days at a time on the fells. It had been more than an escape from the confines of the house. He'd seen more than beauty in the Dales. Like her, he'd found something special, spiritual, uplifting.

Thoughtfully she listened while Cassian continued to answer the hail of questions coming from Adam, speaking to her son as if he were an adult. It disturbed her that Adam was chattering—*chattering!* when he was usually so monosyllabic!—and it disturbed her that Cassian's lazy, deep voice seemed to be soothing her own agitated mind and slowing her movements till she was wafting languidly about the kitchen and catching herself hanging on every improbable word.

But her son was undeniably happy in Cassian's company. And although she might resent Cassian for being the one who'd taken Adam's mind off the bullying, she was grudgingly grateful.

'Sometimes you must have got soaked to the skin, when you wandered off for days on end!' Adam was saying. 'Wasn't that awful?'

'Not often!' laughed Cassian. 'I checked the chickweed. Failing that, the spiders.'

Adam grinned. 'Chickweed?' he scoffed.

'Sure. It closes up if it's going to rain. And spiders are only active in fine weather. If they remake a web around 6—7 p.m., you can be almost sure it'll stay dry. If it's raining and they're altering their web, it'll clear up. You have to read the signs. For instance, a red sunset tells you that dry air is coming. A yellow one indicates it'll be damp. You can read clouds too. I'll show you sometime.'

Sometime, she thought. Another indication that they wouldn't be leaving soon. Her hopes rose.

'Cool! But…what did you eat?' asked Adam, wide-eyed with admiration.

'Trout, usually. You start downstream, place a light close to the water, and the fish come to look. With care, you can flick one out. I'll show you. There's plenty of food if you know where to look. I can lend you a book about finding food in the wild. But make no mistake,' he warned, 'walking the Dales over a period of days is not something anyone can do—not even an adult. I took no risks, Adam. I learnt the lie of the land first, practised and learnt the art of survival till I could light a fire in a howling gale and tell by sound and smell and feel alone where I was.'

'You mean...' Laura eyed him in amazement. 'You were so determined to escape Aunt Enid that you spent weeks preparing yourself?'

'I think it took two years of concentrated effort before I was sure I knew what I was doing,' he said quietly. Then he smiled. 'I wanted to escape, not die! It was wonderful out there on a starlit night,' he mused softly, his face radiating pleasure. 'The silence was awesome.'

Adam moved a little closer to his new hero. Laura watched, her gratitude towards Cassian a little eclipsed by a wary concern. Adam wasn't tough. She didn't want him trying to emulate Cassian.

'Weren't you horribly afraid?' he asked timidly.

Cassian's eyes liquefied with warmth. 'Sometimes. Especially when the night was black and I hadn't reached the shelter I'd chosen. But I always knew where I was heading, and never left anything to chance. I started with small trips, graduated to longer ones. And each success made me stronger, more confident.'

'And...er...' Adam persisted, 'you weren't popular at school.'

Laura held her breath. He'd slipped the question in as if it were casual. Would Cassian see that her son wanted some reassurance about popularity—and help with the bullying?

'No. Because I was different,' Cassian answered gently, and she felt the air slowly sift from her lungs. He'd be kind to Adam, she felt sure. 'Kids don't like people who stand apart. I was categorised along with the boys with National Health glasses and too much weight. We were bullied as a matter of course. It's a very primitive thing, Adam, a caveman attitude. Part of what they call the biological imperative. That means that it's part of our survival instincts. Oddities are rejected to allow survival of the fittest. The world has moved on since Neolithic times, but unfortunately civilisation hasn't always impacted on some primeval brains!' he finished with a grin.

Adam laughed too. 'What did *you* do when you were bullied? Actually *do*?' he asked with an exaggeratedly nonchalant tone which fooled nobody.

Laura stiffened, turning to face the two of them where they were sitting with cosy familiarity on the old sofa. He'd never talked so openly before. He trusted Cassian, she thought in shock. More than *she'd* ever been trusted. Or were mothers naturally ruled out as confidantes?

'I learnt about pain,' Cassian replied ruefully. He smiled down at Adam, his manner relaxed and inviting.

'Nothing else?' her son asked in disappointment.

'Plenty!'

'What?!'

Eagerly, Adam tucked his legs up on the sofa, his body curled against Cassian's. Laura felt her heart lurch. Her son was looking at Cassian as if he held the Holy Grail in the palm of his hands.

'Well, obviously you know that my solutions won't necessarily be yours,' Cassian flattered, and Adam nodded in sage agreement. 'You'll know that you have to decide how to deal with *your* problem and work out what *you* want—'

'To be tough!' Adam blurted out.

Cassian's arm came about Adam's shoulders and he was nodding as if they both had much in common. To Laura's astonishment, Adam reached up a puny arm and boldly felt Cassian's biceps. She couldn't believe what her reserved and shy son was doing. For the life of her, she couldn't recall him ever touching anyone.

But Cassian was incredibly seductive and...touchable. She went pink, thinking how close she had come to breaking her own rules about personal space.

'My decision exactly.'

'Did you, uh…have the same plan as me?' asked Adam tentatively.

Laura could have wept. Her son desperately needed help and she hadn't seen that. All his stubborn insistence that he was fine had been a cover-up. She couldn't bear it.

'You tell me! I chopped wood,' Cassian confided, perhaps deliberately emphasising the muscle definition of his chest by leaning back, his arms behind his head. Shocked to be distracted, Laura found herself mesmerised by his physique, her throat drying in an instant recognition of his visceral appeal. 'I walked miles too,' he reminisced. 'Climbed hills. At first, I puffed like an old steam train, then I graduated to running up them. I heaved rocks about, making dams on the fells where no one could see me fall or fail or yell in frustration. I suppose that's the kind of thing you've decided to do.'

'Yes!' Adam cried with shining eyes.

Laura felt a shaft of pain that her son had seen a glimmer of hope on the horizon. And she hadn't been the one who'd put it there. She felt a tug of admiration for Cassian's technique.

'Thought so.' Cassian yawned. 'Lucky that everything you need is on the doorstep, isn't it? Logs, hills, rocks. Makes getting fit a piece of cake.' He looked up, saw Laura stupidly holding the saucepan as if she'd been welded to the floor, and smiled. 'No time like the present, Adam,' he said briskly, leaping from the sofa. 'You can start flexing those muscles by mashing the potatoes while I fetch something for pudding.'

'Me?' her son's mouth dropped open and Laura was just about to say that she did all the cooking and housework while Adam studied or rested, when he scrambled up and rushed to her side. 'Right. Er…what do I do, Mum?'

'Bash.''

Tight-lipped, she handed him the masher, wordlessly dropped a knob of marge into the pan and added seasoning.

Out of the corner of her eye, while Adam pounded the potatoes with messianic concentration, she saw Cassian tipping fresh raspberries into a dish which he'd hauled from the cupboard.

'Make yourself at home,' she said tartly.

'I am, aren't I?' he murmured.

She gave him a scathing look and inspected the potatoes. Her brows knitted in a frown at the lumps but before she could say anything to Adam, Cassian squeezed himself between them.

'You're doing great,' he enthused, praising her son where she would have criticised. 'Nearly got all the lumps smashed, I see.'

Adam's eyes rounded in dismay. Hastily he pulled the pan towards him and set about reducing the potato to a creamy consistency.

Laura stood transfixed. Cassian had achieved the required result with consummate skill, craftily ensuring that it was Adam himself who'd decided the mash wasn't up to standard.

'Penny?' Cassian murmured, his palm touching the small of her back.

She felt she'd been set on fire. It had been a mere enquiring touch and yet her body had reacted so violently that it seemed her heart might leap from her breast.

And all the while her mind was teeming with new thoughts, excitement mounting as she examined the idea of praise and suggestion as a replacement for criticism—which up to now had been the only method of shaping a child's behaviour that she'd ever known.

It was as if she'd stumbled on treasure. In a way, she had.

Half-turning, her face now inches from Cassian's, she smiled delightedly into his dark, pooling eyes and instantly became light-headed. Joy was unsettling, she thought warily. Then decided to succumb. What the hell.

'My thoughts are worth more than that,' she said happily. She could have danced. Almost did. Her toes wriggled. She grinned. 'Thank you.'

He raised a heavy eyebrow. 'For what?'

Close up, his mouth looked devastatingly sensual. Again she felt the light pressure of his hand on her spine and she had to struggle to remember what they'd been talking about.

With solemn delight, she met his bone-melting stare. It was the revelation that was making her so delirious. And she wanted to keep her new-found knowledge to herself.

'For showing Adam how to make the perfect mash,' she breathed.

'My pleasure.'

There was a brief pressure on her tingling back and then Cassian had moved away, leaving a cold gap she wanted immediately to fill. With him. To have him close, touching her, gazing into her eyes...

'Inspection!' ordered Adam excitedly, banging the pan in front of her.

She was jerked back to reality. 'Wow!' she marvelled. 'Totally smashed mash! Eat your heart out, celebrity cooks of the world!'

'Bread smells fabulous. Fancy some wine?' Cassian enquired, waving a bottle of red at her.

She beamed, feeling suddenly hedonistic. Wine was a luxury. And a wicked indulgence at lunchtime! 'Yes, please!' she said recklessly, knowing she was being silly, but unable to stop herself. After lifting out the golden brown bread, she picked up a serving spoon—and then on an impulse she handed it to the glowing Adam. 'There you go. Pile the potato on top of the mince, add the cheese, grab the oven gloves and push the dish into the oven. It's ready when the cheese is brown and sizzling. I'm going to put my feet up and luxuriate in the high life.'

Flushed and happy, she sat neatly in the armchair while

Cassian opened the bottle. The sunlight danced on the planes of his face. He looked relaxed and at ease and she felt her entire body responding to his mood, softening and slowing down as if she too were laid back and uninhibited.

Her fortunes had changed. Cassian had now met Adam and seen his needs. Instinctively she knew they'd be staying for a while—and perhaps she could even come up with some means of sharing the house till he grew tired of such a narrow world and drifted off to pastures new.

A little fragment of doubt interrupted her plan, a small voice telling her that Cassian wasn't an ordinary man, that she was already disturbed by his deep sensuality. But she could surely curb her mad thoughts if it meant she and Adam could stay at Thrushton.

Perhaps she could cook and clean and do Cassian's washing in addition to holding down a new job. No man would refuse free housekeeping services!

Dreamily planning, she surveyed him from beneath her lashes. With the enjoyment of a true sensualist, he was passing the opened bottle beneath his nose, his face rapt as he inhaled the aroma. Her senses quickened.

Slowly he filled two glasses and carried one over to her. 'Enjoy,' he murmured.

Their fingers touched as she took the glass. A flash of heat melted in the core of her body and she felt Cassian's sharp exhalation of breath warming her lips before he re-treated to the sofa again. She was afraid he was annoyed by her goucheness, but he said nothing. Fortunately, he was totally indifferent to her.

Instead, he concentrated on his wine, quietly studying its colour, sniffing it again and then taking an absorbed sip.

'What do you think of it?' he asked, as if her opinion mattered. He shot her a look and his dark eyes suddenly glowed.

She pressed her parted lips together hurriedly and picked up the glass. 'I don't know anything about wine.'

'You have taste buds!' he growled.

She took a cautious sip. And then another.

'Describe what you feel,' Cassian coaxed.

'I feel warm. From cooking,' she said, ducking the issue and omitting to say that he had added to that warmth.

When he remained silent, she concentrated harder, tasting the rich, dark red wine and trying to find words to explain the glorious sensation in her mouth and the wickedly pleasurable feeling as the alcohol pooled seductively in her stomach.

'I love the smell,' she decided, playing safe. 'It makes me feel rich.'

'Let me sniff, Mum!'

Laughing, she held her glass up to Adam who rolled his eyes and declared he was a millionaire.

'Not far off the truth,' Cassian acknowledged. 'Nothing better than good food and wine, to love and to be loved.'

Laura felt a tightening in her chest. He had someone, she thought, quite irrationally disappointed. It had never occurred to her that the wolf that walked alone would have found a soul mate, but there was no mistaking the depth of emotion in his words. He wore no ring, but then Cassian wouldn't allow any woman to curtail his freedom.

'I've got Mum,' Adam said, treading where angels and she feared to tread. 'Who've you got?'

'My son,' Cassian said softly.

Laura almost spilled her wine. She put it down on the table, her mind whirling. 'Your son?' she repeated stupidly.

'Jai. He's ten.'

'I'm nine!' Adam cried in delight.

Cassian grinned. 'I know. Small world.'

Adam began rattling off questions. Quickly she realised that this was why he'd had such a sure and empathetic touch with her son. Cassian had practical experience of his own.

And what, she thought in quite extraordinary agitation,

about his partner? The woman who'd won his heart, who'd slowly, seductively stripped the clothes from that lithe and lean body...

Laura gulped, appalled at herself. Without any reason whatsoever, she was horribly, stupidly, jealous. She wanted to be close to Cassian...perhaps because it would be wonderful to have the power to conquer someone so quietly strong and independent that his very kiss would be an acknowledgement that she was unique among women. She wanted to sit with him, to be enclosed in his arms and to be soothed by his steady calmness...and to be fired by the passions that lay beneath.

Dear heaven, she thought in horror. What was happening to her?

'Marrakesh?' Adam's exclamation made Laura jump.

Cassian hastily got up and opened the oven door, taking out the pie then prepared a pan for the frozen peas he'd produced. Now *he* was entering into displacement activities. Anything, he thought, to avoid Laura's captivating face as she dreamed of...what?

All he knew was that his willpower was being sorely tested and every nerve in his body was begging him to go over and relieve his desire to kiss her soft mouth till his senses reeled. Suicidal!

'Yes,' he said, waiting for the water to boil and glad of an excuse to keep his back to her. 'Jai's hiking in the High Atlas mountains with friends. They'll put him on a plane to Heathrow and he'll make his way here in a couple of days or so, I'm not sure when.'

There was a deafening silence. Glancing round, he saw that Laura's eyes were nearly falling out of their sockets.

'A ten-year-old, finding his way on his own?' she said in horror. 'Don't you think that's stretching independence too far? Anything might happen to him! There are bad people out there, Cassian—'

'Allow me to know how to manage my own son,' he

said irritably. 'Maybe I've arranged for someone to watch over him. Maybe he's thrilled at the thought of planning his own journey. Maybe he has travelled alone before and has developed strategies to stay safe.' His jaw tightened. How dare she assume he hadn't thought of Jai's safety? 'Maybe,' he said sarcastically, 'I don't care if he's robbed or attacked or abducted by—'

'OK, OK, I'm sorry!' she muttered awkwardly.

He grunted and tipped half the frozen peas into the pan, securing the remainder in the bag with a twist tie. He knew he'd overreacted but no one, just no one, interfered between him and Jai, whose life he'd guard with his own.

'Here,' he growled lobbing the bag at Adam. Who fumbled and dropped them. An easy catch. Poor kid had much to catch up on, he mused and softened his expression. 'Freezer?' he suggested, when Adam looked at him with a puzzled frown.

'Oh, yeah.' The lad disappeared into the scullery and the door banged shut behind him.

He remembered that scullery. He'd stood peeling potatoes for hours there, till his hands were raw. And Laura's father had been furious, Cassian thought darkly, because he'd been unable to break Cassian's will.

Of small victories like that, Cassian knew his character had been forged. And consequently he had his own ideas on how to bring up children. Not by making them peel sacks of potatoes, of course! Gradual responsibility. The acquisition of life skills. Knowledge is power.

Hearing Adam fumbling around in the freezer, he took the opportunity to confront Laura. 'It looks as if we're going to be together for a short while. The shorter the better, I think. But while we are under the same roof, you can keep your thoughts to yourself where Jai is concerned. We have our own way of living and we're happy with it. Any problems, bring them to me. You won't nag Jai and tell him to put his coat on because it's cold. You won't tell him to be careful if he decides to cook. He does what he's capable of. Understand?' he snapped.

'So long as Jai's behaviour doesn't affect Adam,' she said, her eyes wide and anxious.

'Maybe that would be an improvement.'

She bristled, as he knew she would. 'How d—?' Adam walked in again and she broke off, biting her lip. 'How long do you think, before you take those peas off?' she amended, filling in the awkward silence. But her eyes told him how angry she was. And he felt a small leap of triumph.

'Now.'

Cassian spun on his heel and took the pan off the heat for straining. But he was thinking all the while that if he strode over and kissed her passionately on that soft, quivering pink mouth then she might unwind a little. And she and her son might begin to live.

She came to his side, fussing with the plates and he let her take over because otherwise he'd grab her arms and pull her against him so he could rain kisses on her long, slender neck and tousle that perfectly tidy hair.

He wanted to muss her up. To murmur wicked, seductive words in her ear, to rouse her beyond her prim and restrictive responses till she cried out his name and begged for him in husky, unrecognisable tones.

Crazy. The lure of the unattainable. Or perhaps he needed the release of sex. If so, he needed a woman who wanted fun and no strings, not the uptight, emotionally repressed Laura who'd probably expect a ring on her finger if he went so far as to hold her hand.

Grimly he sat at the table. Adam chattered and he answered as best he could. The kiddie had a sweet temperament but was as vulnerable as hell. He itched to set him on the right road. Hated to see a child crushed by life, condemned to feeling inferior to others.

Like Laura. He tore off a piece of crusty new bread and

chewed irritably. She'd annoyed him from the first moment he'd set eyes on her, with her mimsy little voice and breathy uncertainty, scuttling to do the evil Enid's bidding. If his mother hadn't told him to leave Laura strictly alone, he'd have dragged the kiddie off on his attempts to toughen himself up. Though everyone would have imagined they'd been up to no good.

Angrily he replenished Laura's glass and his own. He wasn't used to walking on tiptoe around people and the next few days were going to be foul. It was his habit not to pussyfoot around but to be straight with people. If he did that, he and Laura would be in the sack and Adam would be doing press-ups in the garden each morning.

'Is the pie all right?' Laura's anxious voice impinged on his thoughts.

He looked at his plate and realised he hadn't been eating. 'It's great,' he said honestly, tucking in. 'And the bread is wonderful.'

At least she could cook. That suggested *one* sensual delight in her repertoire.

'I'm glad you like it!'

He looked up and was shaken by her pleased smile. His jaw clenched. She was terrifyingly vulnerable too. One wrong word from him and she could be seriously wounded. It was a hell of a burden to carry.

'I'm going out,' he said when he'd finished. 'Excuse me—'

'But...your pudding!' she cried.

Impatiently he sighed. 'It's not compulsory.'

She flushed and he was back into whipping puppies again. 'But...you haven't even unpacked yet,' she pointed out hesitantly as if he might have forgotten.

'I know,' he bit irritably and she had the grace to look contrite. 'But that can wait and I want to walk.'

Before she could come up with some other conventional chain to wrap around his neck, he strode out.

It wouldn't work, he thought darkly, changing into walking boots and slinging a small rucksack on his back. Laura and he would never live in the same world. Somehow he had to force her out. Before he did something he'd regret for the rest of his life.

Or he could sell up. Perhaps coming here had been a mistake after all.

He set off at a blistering pace, walking off his frustrations.

By the time three hours had passed by, the magic of the fells had made his heart sing again. His route had taken him way beyond the ruined buildings of the medieval lead mines above Thrushton, and past the narrow fourteenth-century hump-backed packhorse bridge with its ankle-high parapets, designed so that a train of forty mules could pass with their laden panniers unimpeded.

Taking delight in treading in the footsteps of history, he walked along the corpse way. He could almost feel the weight of the past, hear the mourners as they carried a loved one to the church, along the narrow path and over the treacherous stepping stones from some remote settlement.

From the track he had climbed high above the beautiful valley where the River Wharfe glinted and sparkled far below and as he climbed he felt a soaring joy at being alive.

The air was sharp and clear and filled with swooping swallows creating a ballet in the air. Overcome by powerful emotions which shook him to the core, he sat on the edge of a limestone pavement, watching an adder drawing the last vestiges of warmth from the late afternoon sun.

He closed his eyes, almost pained by the beauty of his surroundings. And he knew then that he had to spend time here. Wanted... His breath knifed in, snapping his eyes open again. Shock ran through his body. For a brief moment it had crossed his mind that this would be a suitable place to settle. To put down roots.

In a dazed blur, he saw himself creating a herb garden and feeding hens. And then, totally unbalanced by such uncharacteristic dreams, he leapt up and headed at a half-run for Grassington, determined to drink or wench away any potential curbs on his personal freedom.

'I can live here,' he muttered to himself like a mantra, his loping stride swiftly devouring the ground. 'But there's no way I'm going into pipe and slippers mode!'

The beer was good. The women less so. He smiled rue-fully on his way back to Thrushton Hall. Women had rec-ognised him. Fluttered their lashes in the hope that he'd remember their totally unsatisfactory teenage embraces. He'd raised his glass in acknowledgement and remained aloof. The loner.

And despite the attentions of what he assumed to be the landlord's 'bosomy' daughters, he felt nothing; no desire, no stirring, no interest whatsoever.

Worse, he found himself comparing them with Laura. Her quiet beauty. Solemn eyes of cerulean-blue, the colour of a Mediterranean sky. Untouched lips he wanted to explore. The body of a siren and the innocence of an angel.

A woman alone. Unique. Unaware that she was close to spilling out her long-hidden passions and needing someone who wouldn't hurt her, who wouldn't damage her fragile self-esteem but who would build it up till she realised her full potential.

And he wanted to be that man. Even though he knew he couldn't give her what she would want. Marriage. Security. Two point four children and a mortgage and the ritual of cleaning the car every Saturday morning after doing the weekly shop.

So he had to keep his hands and his eyes to himself. And save them both from disaster.

Trying to settle his thoughts, he walked down to the

river, knowing the narrow path so well that the occasional light from the thin crescent moon was enough when the clouds lifted, and so he did not need to use his torch.

He let the soft rush of water soothe his mind. Listened to the scops owl, the sounds of badgers snuffling up roots somewhere in the mid distance. Simple pleasures which money could never buy.

It wasn't until after midnight that he returned, letting himself into the house silently. He took a deep breath to steel himself. Now he would face the house, at its darkest and most sinister and chase away the memories till only stone and mortar remained.

CHAPTER FIVE

LAURA had been unable to sleep. It bothered her that Cassian hadn't stopped to sort out which bedroom he'd use or even unpacked his night things. Did he think he could come back in the early hours and wake her up, demanding sheets and pillows? she thought crossly.

So here she was, having to stay awake to tell him that she'd made up a bed in the back room. It was typically selfish of him that he did his own thing and never mind anyone else!

Her mouth pruned in. That was him now. Grudgingly she admitted that he had been extraordinarily quiet, but she had been waiting for that slight creak of the door, her ears tuned like interstellar radar to an invading Martian.

Flinging her cosy blue dressing gown over her short cotton nightie, she angrily tied the cord around her waist as if girding herself up for battle.

Her head cocked on one side. Instead of coming up the stairs, he was moving around in the dark downstairs. That was the study door opening. Her eyes narrowed. What was he doing?

She listened but there was no sound from below. Then the boards creaked in the hall and there came the unmistakable sound of the latch being lifted on the dining room door.

Well, she thought grimly, if he was looking for money, he'd be disappointed! Curiosity got the better of her and she tiptoed onto the landing, intending to catch him redhanded at whatever he was doing.

At the top of the stairs she froze as Cassian's dark figure crossed the hall beneath her and glided stealthily into the sitting room. With the utmost care she crept down and by the time she peered into the room her nerves were strung along wires.

He stood with his back to her, his bulk just visible in the pale light which filtered through the thin curtains. He seemed to be listening, his very muscles and sinews straining from powerful emotion as he remained rooted to the spot with that deep inner stillness which was peculiar to him.

Laura frowned. Something about him kept her from calling out. He wasn't searching for anything. More like... making a reaquaintance with the house.

She stiffened, her hand going to her mouth as she realised why he was creeping about like a burglar. Earlier on, he hadn't ventured into the rest of the house but had remained in the kitchen, and briefly, the hall.

Intuitively she knew that he must be reliving bad memories. A chill iced her spine.

'Cassian!' she breathed, aching to see what this was doing to him.

But he ignored her because no sound had emerged from her dry throat.

Unaware that he was being watched from the darkness of the hall, he scanned the sitting room with painstaking slowness. Half-turning, his eyes focused on the inglenook and she felt her heart lurch. In the gloom she could see that his face was bleak, his jaw rigid with tension.

'Cassian!' she pleaded in soft concern.

His body jerked. When he swung around she saw with shock that his eyes were silvered and as hard as bullets.

'This is private!' he said fiercely.

She felt like an intruder in her own house. His house. 'But—'

'Don't crowd me! Leave me alone!' he snapped.

Taking a deep breath, his face set, he strode to the fireplace. Picking up a log from the stack, he weighed it in his hand then sniffed its resiny smell. Slowly he returned it to the neatly-stacked pile. Placing his palm on the massive granite lintel across the fireplace, he stared moodily at the hearth.

Laura swallowed, knowing what must be going through his mind. He'd chopped logs in all weathers and had never complained or run to his blissfully unaware mother. Bathsheba was usually engrossed in painting her wonderful landscapes but, even so, Laura had found it hard to understand why Cassian had suffered in silence.

'I chopped those,' she said, desperate to lighten the oppressive atmosphere. 'My axe technique's improved over the years.'

His head lifted but he didn't look at her. 'I'm not in the mood to chat. Please go. I can lock up,' he said icily, his profile taut and uncompromising.

She bristled. 'I thought I'd better wait up because—'

His eyes blazed at her, black and glittering. 'I'm not a child!'

'But I made up a bed for you!' she protested tremulously. 'You wouldn't have known where to sleep...' She stopped, cut short by his irritable sigh.

'It didn't matter. I would have curled up on the sofa,' he said dismissively.

'But you would have been uncomfortable—'

'Laura! That's my problem, not yours!' He paused, gazing at her in consternation. 'I thought you knew me better,' he reproached.

She was shocked by her reaction to his disappointment. She wanted to understand him, to please him. And she had no idea what she'd done wrong.

'Don't live my life,' he went on, his face tight with restraint. 'Don't fit me into your ordered, conventional routine!'

'I was being thoughtful,' she said unhappily.

He looked at her helplessly. 'I know. You were. Hell.

Where do I begin? We both lived in this house for five years and you have no idea about me, do you?'

'We weren't close,' she sulked.

But, she realised to her astonishment, she'd always longed to be.

'OK. It was a misunderstanding. You were being kind—but I had no idea you'd take it on yourself to look after me. I thought—wrongly—that you knew me better and you'd leave me to my own devices. It never occurred to me that you'd prepare a bed for me—so you can't be annoyed with me for keeping you up.'

'No. Suppose not,' she muttered grudgingly.

He sighed. 'I don't know where to begin. Look, I can see it's hard for you to understand how I live—but please don't think you need to run around after me. I've slept on mud floors and bare mountains. I can take care of myself. To be honest, I'm not comfortable with being fussed over. It's...stifling. It's up to me if I eat pudding or not and it's my fault if I'm hungry as a consequence. I'm an adult. If I choose, I can stay out till morning, sleep downstairs or even outside in a field if I want.'

She was beginning to see his point of view. And she had known how independent he was. Unfortunately habit died hard, and the arrival of guests meant looking after them. She'd forgotten that Cassian wasn't an ordinary man.

'I understand,' she said, subdued.

Did he ever need anyone? Flashing into her mind came the unexpected thought that she wanted to care for him, to make him comfortable, happy. But he'd loathe that! She bit her lip and vowed not to push the lone-wolf Cassian into a domestic straitjacket.

'I know I'm difficult, Laura,' he said ruefully. 'I did warn you. I've inherited from my mother an abhorrence of being organised.'

She smiled and lifted bright eyes to his. 'Oh, yes! I remember her yelling at Father about that! I won't do it again.

You can organise yourself in future. But…if you happen
to be passing the back room any time, you'll see I've made
up a bed for you there. You won't have to cosy up to a
sheep tonight,' she said lightly.

'Thank you. I appreciate your trouble. Goodnight.'

He hadn't smiled back at her attempt at levity. His tone
was tight and strained and she knew he wanted to be alone.

'Goodnight,' she said, unwilling to go.

She almost told him what time breakfast would be, but
realised he'd expect to sort himself out. He didn't need
anyone. Especially her.

Upset at that thought, she left the room, her bare feet
silent on the cold stone. Back in the sitting room Cassian
gave a harsh exhalation of breath and she hesitated, her
pulses racing.

'Hell!' he muttered in the silence. His voice had broken
up as if emotion was choking him. 'Give me strength,' he
growled shakily.

Laura was appalled. Was he pleading for strength to cope
with her? She listened, her ears straining in the stillness of
the night.

'You nerd. It's a cupboard,' she heard him mutter.

And her heart seemed to leap to her throat. The cupboard. He'd been banished there more times than she could
remember. It had been unlit then, with a freezing stone floor
and huge spiders.

Cassian was testing himself. That's the kind of man he
was. Before he felt able to stay here, he needed to come to
terms with the harshness of his treatment at Thrushton.

Her eyes darkened as her tender heart went out to him.
And yet…if he did conquer the past then she would definitely find herself without a home. From her point of view
it might be better if Cassian never overcame the bad memories which filled the silent corners of the house.

She could leave him to it. Hope that he discovered he
hated the atmosphere still, and that the reminders of her

adoptive father and her aunt were too powerful even for him to be comfortable with.

But even as that thought raced through her head, she knew she had to help him. His distress cut into her very heart and nothing would stop her from offering solace, not even his scorn or his anger.

Soundlessly, she tiptoed back to the doorway, initially keeping well hidden in the shadows.

As she'd expected, he stood in front of the cupboard, his fists tightly clenched, his shoulders high. A rush of emotion hurtled through her. This had been his hell. And she couldn't just walk upstairs when her soul was reaching out to him in sympathy.

Quietly she crossed the soft carpet and stood so close to him that their arms touched. For a moment it seemed that he leaned nearer, though she might have been the one to do so. The fact that he hadn't yelled at her was encouraging and she even believed that his tense muscles had relaxed a little.

'Don't do this, not now,' she whispered into the thick, cloying silence.

'I must.'

Stricken by his choked reply, she astonished herself by putting an understanding hand on his increasingly rigid back. Looking up at him, she saw that his jaw was set and his eyes seemed distant as if he remembered every incident, each indignity, the slaps and the punishments which had made up his days.

With a suddenness that took her by surprise, he lurched forwards and wrenched open the cupboard door. The breath became strangled in her throat. His face was white and he was sweating, beads of perspiration standing out on his forehead.

Her fist went to her mouth. 'Oh, Cassian!' she whispered.

He didn't speak. For a long, agonising time he stared into the black recesses of the deep cupboard and she relived her own terror of all those years ago when he'd nonchalantly walked in there, his head held high in defiance as if he were entering a paradise.

The hackles rose on the back of Laura's neck. For the freedom-loving Cassian this must have been a terrible ordeal.

Seconds ticked past and his facial muscles tightened till she couldn't bear it. 'Cassian—'

'Shut me in.'

She jerked in a shocked breath. *'What?'*

'Do it.'

He stepped in and turned, his eyes commanding her.

'No!' she breathed in horror.

He glowered, his jaw clenched. 'Do it!' he commanded.

She gulped. And knew she must. Mesmerised, she clasped the latch in a shaking hand and slowly closed the door. Aghast, she stared at the oak panels with wide, anxious eyes. For several long minutes she waited, cold and shivering, her pulse thundering in her ears as she imagined what must be going through his mind.

There was a light knock on the door. With relief she stumbled forwards to open it again and Cassian emerged: shaking, breathing heavily, but with the light of triumph in his eyes. Laura gave a little cry and ran to him, briefly hugging him before moving back in confusion.

'You're freezing!' he said with a frown. He reached out and rubbed her arms.

'I'm all right,' she croaked, still reeling from the feel of his strong body against hers. 'Are you?'

'Fine.'

His hands were slowing and warmth was flowing into her—though it was nothing to do with any external temperature. She picked off spider threads from his shirt and suddenly felt overcome with the intimacy of such an action.

'I was just worried about you,' she babbled.

'I was OK. I'll put a key on the inside so no one can ever be locked in. It's all in the past, now.'

'I really didn't want to shut that door. It wasn't your favourite place of all time. Was it really awful, being locked in there when you were a kid?' she asked, and could have kicked herself for such stupidity. Of course it had been awful.

'It was a lesson.'

Puzzled, her small face lifted to his. And she saw the strength there, the fierce willpower which she had always admired and envied.

'In what?' she asked in awe.

'Detachment. Mind over matter.'

'But you must have dreaded going in there each time,' she persisted, for some reason wanting him to acknowledge the horror of sitting in a small, dark cupboard on a solid stone floor for hours on end.

'Sometimes, Laura,' he said huskily, 'you have to face your fears to become stronger.'

'But…' Her face grew perplexed. 'Everywhere you look in this house you must see things you'd rather forget.'

'If you can live here,' he said softly, 'so can I.'

'I'm different—'

'You can say that again,' he murmured wryly.

She flushed, wishing they weren't light years away from one another. But persisted with her point. 'We are total opposites. You and your mother were like…like wild birds!' she exclaimed. 'You both craved freedom! I, however, have always been tractable—'

'Laura. Don't be mistaken; we are all passionate about the things we love.' His hot, dark eyes burned into hers till the breath came short and fast in her throat and she could feel the increased pressure of his hands around her arms. 'Even you. You are passionate about your son—'

'Am I?' she breathed in amazement.

'Fiercely. Your love for him overrides everything else.'

His smile dazzled her, sending her nerves into a tailspin. 'As for me, I don't know why I have to be here, only that I felt an irresistible pull the moment Tony mentioned the house. And,' he went on huskily, 'when I saw the sun on the fells, glinting on the drystone walls and Thrushton nestling on the slopes, my heart leapt in my body. I need to be here and I will come to terms with my past. That is just a cupboard and it holds no terrors for me any more. I must live here to make this house ordinary in my mind again. I think it's part of my rites of passage.'

She grasped that, but would never fully understand him, she thought, stunned by how sad that made her feel. She would never know what drove him, pleased him, made him tick. Would never reach the impenetrable depths which made him so fascinating and desirable.

The past and the present collided. Tension had torn at her nerves making them raw. Cassian always unsettled her, turned her life upside down, upset her. She began to cry silently but didn't know why, and turned away blindly so that he didn't suspect.

But he knew. His hands were on her shoulders, strong, firm, comforting. Gently he coaxed her around and then suddenly she seemed to be crushed against him, weeping quietly into his shoulder.

'I—I'm sorry!' she mumbled in dismay, trying to pull back. He resisted her efforts and she was secretly glad. 'I shouldn't—'

His finger lifted her chin and she did her best to stop her stupid sobbing. 'If you need to cry, then cry,' he said softly. 'There's no point in bottling it up.'

There was. Miserably she blinked in a heroic effort to stem the flood, her tongue desperately mopping up any tears which headed near her mouth. Something told her that if she really let go, then all her carefully constructed world would start falling apart.

'I have to stay in control!' she mumbled.

'Why?'

'Of course I must! Everyone should! Where'd we be otherwise?' she said wildly.

'Laura!' he husked.

His hand slid around to cradle her jaw. Through the veil of tears she could see that his eyes were bright, his lips parted in consternation.

There was a tenderness in his expression which made her heart lurch. Suddenly she felt giddy, as if she were being lifted off her feet by a whirling wind and carried into the sky. Her eyes seemed to be closing of their own accord. The sensation persisted, even intensified and she had the impression that there was no solid ground beneath her feet any more.

She could smell him. A wonderful, alien, male smell that tantalised her nostrils and increased the beat of her heart. Beneath her palms his chest was firm, the pressure of his body a delight.

A soft sigh escaped her as she revelled in the contrast between his masculine strength and her own soft yielding.

'Cassian,' she found herself murmuring.

His embrace enfolded her more securely and she felt an extraordinary elation. Although she was intensely aware of her nakedness beneath the robe and thin cotton nightdress it didn't bother her.

Drowsily her eyes opened. A sudden rush of warm breath raced over her face and she tensed expectantly, straining upwards for the wonderful moment when their mouths would meet.

'Would you...?'

Laura smiled invitingly, delighted by his huskiness. 'Mmm?' she prompted gently.

He cleared his throat. 'Would you like my handkerchief or are you all right now?' he shot out.

They both stepped back from one another; Cassian's expression unreadable, hers transparent with disappointment till she managed to haul the shreds of her tattered dignity about her again.

'I'm OK,' she lied jerkily, avoiding his horribly perceptive eyes.

OK? Her whole body was screaming for him, like a child having a tantrum because it has been deprived of a favourite toy.

'I don't know why I cried—' she mumbled.

'You don't need a reason. Or to give me one,' he said softly.

'I'm not a wimp—' she began.

'I know. I think you're brave.'

She met his eyes then, and found herself caught by them. 'Brave?' she squeaked, feeling her body reaching melting point again.

'Strong, too, and determined. It can't have been easy, bringing up Adam on your own with Enid presumably breathing fire and brimstone and calling all kinds of damnation on your head.'

She gave a wry smile. 'It was a bit like that.'

'You could have given him up for adoption,' he suggested.

'Never!' she declared in horror. 'He was my baby! I loved him from the start. I'd have sooner cut out my heart than give him away!'

'I thought so,' he said gently. 'Laura, I want you to listen to me very carefully. This is important.'

He was smiling at her. She responded with one of her own and was thrilled when she saw a glow light up his eyes.

Kiss me, she told him, with every ounce of her being.

'I'm listening,' she said, deceptively demure. And intensely hopeful.

Cassian touched his lips with the tip of his tongue and Laura swallowed, her eyes huge with longing.

'I believe in Kismet. Fate,' he said thickly.

It had brought him here. 'Me too,' she breathed, her face radiant.

Tight-jawed, he folded his arms, a gesture which immediately put a barrier between them. Laura's hopes and dreams began to fade.

'My arrival releases you,' Cassian said, still hoarse, but perhaps with embarrassment and not desire.

Laura stared in dismay, her mouth suddenly unruly and refusing to obey when she tried to stop it quivering.

'From…what?' she mumbled with difficulty.

'Everything that's kept you here. For you,' Cassian continued more curtly, 'the next journey in life is to shake off the shackles of this house and this village and to take your son and yourself somewhere new.'

'No!' she cried in horror.

He frowned down at her, no longer someone she could trust, but a cold and determined stranger.

'You are strong and you are brave, and your devotion to Adam will ensure that you both survive. I know you can do it,' he rasped. 'I'll give you a week to tell Adam and to get used to the idea. After that, you're out on your ear.'

CHAPTER SIX

THE sound of music woke her, seeping through the house with a soft insistence. Glancing in outrage at the bedside clock she saw it was only six-thirty.

Wretched Cassian! She needed that extra half-hour after tossing and turning all night, seething with anger at how badly she'd misread Cassian's intentions! Far from being close to kissing her, he'd been searching for a way to tell her she wasn't welcome in his house.

And now she was horribly, thoroughly awake.

Muttering under her breath, she dived into the bathroom and showered, dressed and made her bed all in record time. And apart from the few moments when she wielded her toothbrush with unusual vigour, her teeth were angrily clamped together for the whole fifteen minutes.

As she passed Adam's room, she saw that the bed was already made. That meant Cassian had woken him too!

Determined to lay down a few ground rules before putting over her housekeeping plan, she stomped down the stairs, astonished to be met by the delicious smell of bacon.

And then she was confronted by the shocking sight of Adam, scarlet in the face—a fever, perhaps—and yet he was checking the six rashers sizzling gently on the grill which he was holding at a very careful arm's length.

She gasped. He was ill. Alone. Cooking without supervision! Of all the reckless, thoughtless...

'Adam!' she exclaimed. 'What the—?'

'Hi, Mum! Shall I do you some?'

She didn't know where to begin her tirade. She identified the source of the music. It came from a small, state of the art personal stereo. The wonderful swelling sound was

87

washing gently through her brain, doing its best to soothe
her temper.

But she wouldn't be placated. First she'd deal with
Adam's fever. Then she'd find Cassian and flay him alive.

'Sweetheart, your face is terribly flushed,' she said boss-
ily. 'I ought to take your temperature—'

'Morning, Laura. He's fine, it's only a healthy glow.
We've been out for a run,' came Cassian's voice from the
scullery beyond. 'Found some mushrooms on the way,' he
added, coming into the kitchen.

Laura's eyes popped. True to his earlier threat, he was
wearing nothing but a bath towel! Acres of tanned, muscular chest speedily impressed themselves on her retinas so
indelibly that she wondered if she'd ever find room for any
other vision again.

'M-morning!' she gasped.

'Chanterelles, parasols, ceps. Not bad. I've brushed them
clean,' he said to Adam, casually adding the mushrooms to
the grill and drizzling on a few drops of oil.

She blinked, all the better to clear her fogged eyes and
brain and to see the interesting movements of muscle beneath the flawless back, which was so smooth and glowing
that she could hardly hold back from reaching out to caress
it.

Briefly she let her gaze wander to the narrow hips and
the small, tight rear beneath the thin, clinging towel. It was
an awful mistake. Terrible things were beginning to happen
to her. Delicious sensations. Wicked yearnings.

But sex-god or not, her boring, Aunt-Enid generated
conscience told her sternly, this man was ruthless and heartless and she'd better not forget that.

'Now Cassian—!' she began angrily, all set for a show-
down.

'Just a sec—' He wasn't paying her any attention, his
alert and watchful eyes constantly on Adam. 'Looks great,

steady as she goes,' he said in his deep, calming voice, leaning nonchalantly against the Aga rail.

'Will the sausages pop?' Adam asked nervously.

'Not on the simmer plate. You've got a splatter guard, anyway. Just show them you're the boss. The pan will be safe and steady if you hold the handle firmly.'

'Like that?' Adam assumed a more commanding position.

'Perfect,' beamed Cassian. 'It's like everything; success is a matter of application and keeping focussed on the task.'

'The sausies look a bit brown on their bottoms,' Adam said uncertainly.

'You're right.' Cassian handed him the tongs.

Laura sullenly admired his technique. He hadn't said the sausages needed turning, but had waited till Adam had noticed that fact for himself. The edges were rubbed off her anger. She couldn't help but be impressed by Cassian, callous brute though he may be.

She sat down, non-plussed, her gaze sliding surreptitiously back to him as he raised a hand and slicked back his hair which was still wet and shiny from his shower. Absently he rubbed his damp palm on his rear. No noticeable wobble. Taut muscles. Small and neat...

Laura tried to breathe normally. She couldn't cope with so much nakedness, so much male beauty. It was too early. And to make matters worse, she had the distinct feeling that she was being superseded.

A sausage sizzled menacingly as Adam wielded the tongs. And she jumped up again.

'Cassian! The fat—!' she cried in alarm.

'Sound effects, nothing more,' Cassian said airily. 'There's virtually no fat at all, the way we're cooking. He's safe, I promise you.'

She glared. If her son was burned, she'd...

'Great grub, isn't it?!' enthused Adam, failing dismally to turn any of the sausages.

She took a step to help but felt a heavy hand descend on her shoulder pushing her back into the chair. Cassian's carefully draped towel brushed her leg. His hip was an inch from her eyes and she almost craned her neck to follow the delicious aroma of fresh soap that had accompanied his sudden movement.

'Little beggars, sausies, aren't they?' sympathised Cassian, releasing his hold on Laura. 'Oh, well done. They give in eventually. One down, three to go.'

Her mouth opened and closed. The burning imprint of his hand remained on her shoulder.

'What was this about a run?' she queried icily.

She peered hard at Adam for signs of exhaustion. There were none. That should have pleased her but it made her crosser than ever and she felt horribly guilty because of that.

'Cassian asked if I'd like to go with him. We were up before six,' Adam said proudly. 'We walked and jogged and ran then walked and jogged and ran,' he explained. 'It's a good way to start exercise. I could have gone on,' he boasted, 'but Cassian said he was starving so I agreed to come back.'

'Oh, yes?'

Laura's cynical glance made Cassian grin and shrug his shoulders in amusement behind Adam's absorbed back. Cassian was so fit he could have run to London and back without breaking into a sweat. But at least, she thought, Cassian had been careful not to drive her son to the limit of his endurance.

'This is a first. You never eat breakfast,' she pointed out to her son, having tried for years to interest him in more than a meagre slice of toast and a glass of orange.

It annoyed her that Adam didn't answer. He was occupied in looking blankly at the egg which Cassian had handed to him as if he'd never seen one.

'I'll do the first, you do the next,' Cassian murmured,

sotto voce. 'Watch. Small tap with a knife, fingers in carefully, open it up very slowly...break it into this cup and tip
it into the poacher.'

He was behaving like a conspirator, Laura thought huff-
ily. For the first time in her life, she was playing second
fiddle to someone else in Adam's life. And she couldn't
bear it.

To her amazement, Adam managed the tricky operation
and grinned up at Cassian in delight, receiving a slap on
the back.

'Eggsellent!' Cassian said with a grin.

Laura looked at her giggling son as if he'd betrayed her.
'So now you're a fan of cooked breakfasts,' she said lightly,
trying to keep the scouring jealousy out of her tone.

'I didn't have the benefit of fresh air and exercise before,' he said absently.

He pushed back a blond hank of hair with a busy hand
and cracked another egg with great success. It was as if
he'd scored a goal for Manchester United.

'Hey! How about that?' he cried in delight, taking a bow.

'Brilliant,' conceded Laura, squirming at his pleasure.
This wasn't her son. It just wasn't.

Cassian put an arm around Adam's shoulder. They
looked very much at home with one another. Her eyes
clouded.

'There's plenty for you, Laura,' murmured Cassian, 'if
you want some. I bought loads.'

She could be proud and stick to toast and marmalade, or
give in to her hysterical taste buds.

'Thanks,' she said stiffly, managing a compromise. 'I'll
do myself some in a moment.'

She stalked over to the fridge for the juice and stood in
amazement at the sight that met her eyes.

'Is this...yours?' she asked Cassian, overwhelmed by the
amount of food crammed into the small space.

'And yours. I just grabbed a few things on my way here.'

'Few?' Steaks. A joint of lamb, chocolate eclairs…
'We…we can't—'

'Oh, Mum!' complained Adam. 'We can! It can be his
rent for staying here, can't it?'

Her teeth ground together. 'You answer that,' she said
sweetly to the amused Cassian.

'The food is for us. My contribution to the well-being of
our stomachs,' he fudged, his eyes mocking.

'Sending us off into the blue, well-fed?' she queried
waspishly, prompting him to come clean about his presence
in the house.

He smiled and didn't rise to her bait. 'With all the exercise Adam's intending to take, he'll need plenty of sus-
tenance,' he said easily.

'It's brilliant having you here, Cassian. And isn't this
music triff, Mum?' Adam declared, going off at a tangent
and totally oblivious to Laura's fury. 'Andean pipes.
S'posed to sound like condors, soaring over mountain
peaks. Condors are big birds of prey, Mum.'

'Are they?' she replied drily.

But she lifted her head and listened to the music, hearing
the sound of wind on feather, the chillingly beautiful echo
of the pipes—as if they were rebounding from one mountain top to another.

She was aware of Cassian watching her intently and lowered her gaze, annoyed to be caught out enjoying the music
and disturbed that her senses had been so deeply stirred.

'I've made Turkish coffee for myself. Want to try some?'
he murmured.

Even now, though she knew his intentions towards her—
eviction—her body trembled at the sound of his low, me-
lodious voice. Even, she thought, wryly, at the crack of
dawn.

If he could have this kind of effect on her, in a kitchen,
with the smell of sausages pervading the air, what could he

achieve over a candlelit dinner for two and a splash of aftershave?

'All right,' she said with a shrug.

Cassian poured some treacly liquid into a small cup from an exotic-looking silver jug with a beaked nose.

'Do you think everything's done now?' he asked Adam innocently.

'Um...yes, I reckon so,' he replied, flushing with pleasure at being given the responsibility to decide.

Laura shrank into herself even further. The two of them dished up and carried their heaped plates to the table. All very cosy, very intimate and chummy. Laura sat sipping the rich, sweet coffee, feeling utterly miserable and gooseberryish.

They chattered, she was quiet. Adam didn't slump as usual, or eat at a snail's pace. And he looked Cassian directly in the eye, instead of that hesitant, sideways glance he normally gave to people.

It was astonishing. In a few hours, her son had changed. A few culinary skills, a jog across the fields, and he'd gained in confidence.

A sharp pain sliced through her and she hastily got up to cook herself some breakfast. She was a failure. Adam had needed a father—or at the very least, a different mother, she thought, racked with guilt. But she'd done everything she could to protect him. Cared for him, sacrificed much. Why then, should she feel deeply inadequate?

Miserably she looked up, hearing Cassian offer her son a lift to school. She almost told Adam to do his teeth but daren't, not with Cassian's dark eyes upon her in warning.

'I'll go and do the gnashers,' Adam declared. 'Um... what do I need today?' She opened her mouth to reply, but closed it again around a piece of sausage, waiting for her son to work that one out for himself. Perhaps because he wasn't used to doing that, there was a long pause. 'I'd better check what lessons I've got and get my stuff together,' he said eventually. 'Then I can do some extra work on my project till it's time to go.'

'Mmm,' she enthused, and gave him a beaming smile of encouragement. 'You do that, darling.'

Adam dashed out and Cassian raised his coffee cup to her in admiring salute. Laura only just managed to stop herself from blushing coyly and joining the Cassian United Fan Club. But she knew how Adam felt, she mused. Heady, happy, pleased.

She glared at the seductive triangle of Cassian's back. He was already clearing dishes and running water for washing up, his feet planted firmly apart on the stone flags as he tested the temperature of the water and squirted in some of the ecologically friendly washing up liquid he'd bought.

Nice feet, she couldn't help but noticing. Well-shaped, with no ugly lumps or bumps. And muscular calves...

Furious with herself for finding him so attractive, she leapt up and stacked plates on the counter, then grabbed a tea towel. All madly domesticated, she thought grimly.

'Now, look,' she snapped. 'We need to talk.'

'Shall we save it till Adam's at school?' he suggested amiably, working away at an eggy plate.

'No! I can't wait! Now!' she hissed.

'You could shout at me more easily if he's not around,' Cassian pointed out, infuriatingly right.

Laura hauled in a huge breath, ready to explode, but she heard Adam thundering down the stairs and shot Cassian a vicious scowl instead.

'All right. Later,' she grated.

'Look forward to it,' Cassian murmured.

'Hey! I just had a thought,' Adam said excitedly, gazing at Cassian with a hopeful expression. 'Do you know anything about Ancient Egypt?'

'Lived in Cairo and Aswan for a couple of years,' Cassian replied and smiled at Laura when she let out a quiet snort. 'What do you need to know?' he asked Adam.

And soon they were both huddled over Adam's project, with fascinating stories being faithfully recorded—stories so well-told and interesting that Laura found herself moving quietly so that she didn't miss a word.

There were tales of Pharaohs, of greed and ambition, murder and achievement—all woven into a tapestry of facts and figures which made them seem all the more believable.

He was amazing. A walking encyclopaedia, she thought, deciding that everything he said was probably true. A devastatingly charismatic man—and already Adam had fallen under his spell.

She couldn't blame him. If she didn't know Cassian's intentions, she'd be sitting goggle-eyed at his feet, too.

Seeing her child's awe-struck face and shining eyes, she knew that he'd be terribly hurt when Cassian revealed that he owned Thrushton Hall. And she couldn't bear to see Cassian leading Adam on. If they did have to leave, then Adam would find it hard to deal with Cassian's two-faced betrayal.

'Time you went, darling,' she said, sounding choked. 'Got everything?'

'Oh, Mum—!'

'Come on,' Cassian said cheerfully. 'Plenty of time tonight to do a bit more after we've had our run.'

'Another?' Adam looked shocked. 'I usually watch TV—'

Cassian shrugged. 'Whatever you prefer—'

'Oh, a run!'

Laura glared. This was hero worship on a grand scale and it had to stop. '*After* your normal homework,' she put in quickly.

'I knew that!' protested Adam.

And Laura felt a shock go right through her. He was annoyed with her, for the first time in his life.

'I suppose I'd better get dressed,' Cassian said loudly. 'I

imagine towels aren't usually worn on the school run. Be down in a moment.'

'Sorry, Adam,' she said quietly, when Cassian had bounded up the stairs two at a time. 'I shouldn't have nagged.'

'It's OK, Mum. I usually need reminding.' They smiled at one another, friends again, both confused by the small crack in their relationship. 'Isn't he fab, Mum?' Adam enthused.

'Fab,' she managed with a smile.

And suddenly the future seemed even more uncertain than ever. If they left, they'd have problems adjusting to a new and hostile world. If they stayed...

She bit her lip. She'd have to watch her own child worshiping the ground Cassian walked on. She wouldn't be needed any more. The truth was, that Cassian had the advantage of maleness. They'd do men's things together.

And Cassian's extraordinary magic would act as a magnet to the impressionable Adam. She had no fascinating experiences, no exotic background or a storyteller's gift.

She just loved her child. And, she thought forlornly, it seemed that wasn't enough any more.

It was a long time before Cassian returned. She kept looking at the clock, wondering when he'd come back and rehearsing what she'd say.

Everything had been dusted twice, all surfaces wiped down, cobwebs whisked away. The house gleamed and smelt deliciously of lavender but it felt empty and silent after the chatter of the early morning.

Prompted by the deathly quiet, she fiddled with Cassian's stereo and managed to make it eject the condor music and accept something called 'Flames of Fire'.

The house throbbed to a deep and intensely sensual music that sent shivers down her spine and made her think unwisely of Cassian's warm eyes and erotic mouth.

Catching herself breathing more heavily than her recent bout of dusting should have produced, she decided to swap the flames of fire for something that didn't make her erogenous zones tingle. Like a party political broadcast. But she never made the switch.

'You there, Laura? I'm home!'

She stiffened at Cassian's voice, coming from the hall. 'Oh, no, you're not!' she muttered under her breath. This was her home. He merely owned it.

'What do you think of the music?' he asked cheerfully, immediately seeming to fill the sitting room with energy.

'I was just going to turn it off,' she grumped.

'Do that. And get smartened up. I'm taking you off to look for a job.'

Her mouth tightened stubbornly. 'I want to talk to you first—'

'Do it on the way.' He waited expectantly.

She tossed her head in defiance. 'Don't boss me around! I don't like being organised any more than you do—'

'But you need a job.'

'I can go on the bus,' she said, cutting off her nose to spite her face. A lift would have been marvellous. But not with *him*.

'Seems silly. I'm going anyway. So if you don't come with me, your heart to heart talk will have to wait till tonight.' He smiled at her sulky face. 'Come on. You might as well use me, mightn't you? And think of the yelling you can do, while I'm driving.'

He was utterly impossible! She glared. 'Put like that...'

With a show of reluctance, she stalked over to the door, expecting him to move aside. He didn't, and clearly wasn't intending to. The stereo whispered out a deeply passionate refrain that made her entire body contract.

Summoning up all her willpower, she slid past Cassian, totally, intensely aware of the feel of his moleskin trousers, the softness of his brushed cotton shirt, the flurry of warm breath that disturbed her hair…and her senses.

Hot and flustered, she scurried up the stairs. Her heart pounded as she scrabbled out of her clothes and dug out her interview suit. Bottle-green, second-hand and badly fitting. Crisp shirt, well-polished court shoes, well-worn. Ditto handbag.

Smooth the mussed-up hair. How had that happened? Cold water on face. Done.

He was waiting outside. Took one look at her—clearly disapproving, from the quick frown—and opened the passenger door without a word.

Composed now, she climbed onto the high step, hampered by her skirt. Cassian gave a brief push on her bottom and she slid into the comfortable seat pink with embarrassment but determined to use her time usefully.

'I have a proposition,' she announced briskly as they pulled away.

'Uh-huh.'

'You know all the reasons I want to stay.'

'Yup.'

Her hands fidgeted nervously in her lap. Cassian reached over to her side and she flattened herself against the back of the seat. With a curious look at her, he turned on the radio and pushed in a cassette.

Laura groaned. Loin-stirring flamenco music.

'Well,' she said stiffly, 'I've thought of a way to solve the problem.'

Cassian didn't look too pleased about that. 'Oh?' he grunted.

'You can live at Thrushton Hall.'

'Thanks. I'm with you so far,' he drawled.

She took a deep breath. The next bit was tricky.

'I get a job, stay at Thrushton too—and pay rent, and I do all the housework and cooking and washing for you!'

She looked at him anxiously. The signs weren't good. Beetled brows, furrowed brow, tight mouth.

'One teeny flaw. I don't need a housekeeper or a cook or someone to do my washing,' he declared.

Her heart sank. She felt stupid for not realising. Cassian would bring over his woman to Thrushton. It was too painful to contemplate.

'I'd forgotten. You've got your wife. Partner. Whatever,' she floundered miserably.

'No wife, partner or whatever. My wife died when Jai was born,' he snapped.

Now she'd hurt him. 'I'm sorry,' she mumbled.

'Laura, please try to tune in to the kind of man I am. I've always looked after myself. I need no woman for that.' His glance seared into her. 'I've never needed a woman for anything other than love.'

Love. He had sounded very sad as if he was remembering the woman he'd adored so much that he'd risked his love of freedom and gone willingly into marriage. And his wife had died tragically. How awful.

There was a long silence. Then timidly she ventured again.

'You and Jai would be alone?'

'It's how we like it.'

'But I could save you from doing domestic things. They're boring. You'd have more freedom,' she enlarged, 'if you didn't have to do chores—'

'You're very persistent.'

'It's very important!' she replied. 'Well?'

'No.'

Her stomach lurched at the finality of his tone. 'Why not? You hate restrictions! Shopping and cooking—'

'I don't shirk responsibility,' he corrected. 'I just don't do things that are unnecessary.'

'Please, think about it—' she begged, horrified that her great plan had been so casually rejected.

'No.'

She pressed her fist to her mouth and tried to stop the tears of disappointment. She'd really failed this time. For a moment she contemplated the abyss that was her future.

It would be terrible. She felt sick. Adam would be devastated. Her head jerked up. Adam!

'In that case…' She choked, swallowed, and tried to find her voice again. 'In that case,' she cried hotly, 'if we're out on our ears at the end of the week, then leave Adam alone! Don't get close to him!' The flamenco rose to a crescendo and she found herself shouting angrily over the fiery beat. 'You'll destroy him, Cassian! You're not blind. You can see he thinks you're Mr Wonderful. You sit there, telling him stories, behaving like—like a *father* to him, the father he's always wanted, and yet in a few days' time you'll be rejecting him! You can't do that!' she stormed, beating her fists on her knees. 'You can't hurt him, I won't let you…' She broke off. He was pulling over, driving onto the verge. 'What are you doing?' she flared.

'Out.' He jerked his head at her.

Her mouth dropped open. 'You don't mean—?'

'No, I'm not abandoning you,' he said wearily. 'But this is important and I can discuss this more easily when I don't have to concentrate on the road.'

'Discuss?' she raged, half-falling out of the car in her eagerness to get out before he helped her. 'There's no point in talking! You won't listen to me. You don't care what happens to Adam and me. You have no heart! It doesn't matter that he'll be distraught because his god has turned out to have feet of clay and that—'

'Laura!' Cassian was shaking her, his grip firm on her arms. 'Laura, *I do care!*'

CHAPTER SEVEN

HE COULDN'T believe he'd admitted that. He felt her freeze, every muscle, every breath in her body halted by his claim.

'What?' she whispered, searching his face.

'I care about Adam,' he said shortly, and released her. 'Come and sit in the sun.'

'I'm all right here!' she yelled.

'As you wish.'

Touched by her wonderful stubbornness, he settled himself on the low stone wall and stared out at the valley, hoping his inflamed senses would simmer down.

Laura had been more passionate than he could have believed possible. Yesterday he'd watched her responding to the music and enjoying the wine, an excitement surging within him as he saw her long overdue awakening to the pleasures in life.

His body had known little rest since. It demanded that he should introduce her to the greatest pleasure of all.

His eyes closed to the warmth of the sun, feeling his very bones melt at the thought of making love to Laura. Despite the terrible green suit.

'Cassian.'

There was a lurch in his loins. She had come to sit near him.

'Mmm?' he grunted.

'If you care—'

'It's because I care, because I see a child longing to be part of the hurly-burly of the world,' he said grimly, determined to deny himself the pleasure he wanted, 'that I'm determined to extract you both from your shell. He must

take his life in his own hands. He's desperate to be liked
at school. I've never seen a kiddie so anxious to please—'

'What do you mean?' she demanded, suddenly alert.
'Something happened, didn't it? Tell me!' she cried, grabbing his arm with both hands.

He glanced quickly at her fiery eyes and only just managed to drag his gaze away and fix it on a distant peak.

'Oh, some kids making fun—'

'Of Adam?' she cried, aghast.

He sighed, and decided he'd better explain. 'They were
actually pointing at—and mocking—what they imagined to
be my rucksack. It's orange, you see. Day-Glo. So I got
out and told them it was my paraglider and offered to show
it to them.'

She frowned. 'You mean those parachutes with a sort of
strap seat thing beneath it? You fling yourself off mountains
for fun?'

'Something like that.' He was amused by her description
of one of the most exhilarating sports in the world. To fly.
To soar into the sky, to stay airborne by reading the con-
tours of the ground and assessing the thermals… Breathtaking. 'It's a little more complicated, but that's the general
idea,' he acknowledged.

'Then what happened?' she asked curiously.

Bedlam. He grinned and played the whole thing down.

'We got quite a crowd around us. I answered questions
about it and then a woman with a letterbox mouth came
over and told us all off for not hearing the bell.'

'Miss Handley,' Laura said, her mouth curving into a
reluctant smile.

'Yes. The Head. I apologised, said it was all my fault
and why and before I knew what was happening, she had
me in there giving a talk during her assembly.'

Cassian watched a sparrowhawk spill out the air from its
wings, mastering thermals without knowing how.

'I can imagine.' To his relief, Laura sounded drily

amused. Then she frowned. 'I suppose Adam is madly impressed.'

And he sighed. Even now he felt upset by Adam's pitiful delight to be associated with someone 'cool'.

'Adam helped me with my talk,' he said in a low tone. 'Unwrapping my wing. The parachute,' he explained. 'He sat in the seat while I held it.'

He didn't want to say any more. He could see the child's face, bright with joy to be regarded with such envy by the entire school while he talked of flying with black vultures over Spain and with the condors in South America. It hurt him to remember.

Laura was silent. He was glad, needing time to push some steel into his backbone because somewhere a little voice was becoming more insistent, saying that Laura's solution was workable, that he could help them both.

Then common sense reasserted itself. He wasn't God. Shouldn't meddle. She had to find her own way. All he should do was to put her on the road.

Dippers bobbed about on the rocks in the turbulent river below. A heron flapped lazily across the meadow. Far in the distance he could see that a deer had become trapped in a field, enclosed by the high stone walls.

It ran up and down in panic, unsure how it had got there, incapable of finding its way back to safety. He realised that this was what he was doing to Laura and Adam: flinging them into an alien space where there were no recognisable landmarks. Yet, like the deer, they wanted to hide in safety—

'There's a deer trapped!' she cried with concern. And she pointed.

'I know.'

'I forgot. You don't miss a thing, do you?' she said ruefully. 'It's scared, Cassian. Can't we go down the valley and help it somehow?'

'No.'

'Surely we must—'

'Laura, I hate to see it so frightened but we'd scare it even more if we started waving our arms and trying to get it back to the wood. It could hurt itself on the wall—break a leg, perhaps in its panic. Or get caught up in the barbed wire at the top end of the field.'

'It looks so frightened,' she said in a small voice.

He laid his hand on hers. 'It must find its own way,' he said gently.

And, extraordinarily, he wanted to keep Laura safe with him, and not send her out into the wide world. His jaw clenched. He was just missing Jai. Needed company. Someone to hold.

'What is it?' Laura asked softly.

'Jai.' His voice was choked with emotion.

He knew she nodded, though he kept staring straight ahead.

'You're a very caring man. Jai is very lucky to have you as a father.'

He sought her eyes then, almost faltering at the beauty of her misted blue gaze.

'A callous brute like me?' he joked.

She smiled wistfully. 'I know you think you're doing the right thing—that you believe it's "good" for us,' she breathed.

Her face lifted to his, the wind ruffling her hair. And he felt his heart lurch. She was entering his very bones. Shaking the cells in his body. It was purely a yearning for the softness of a woman, nothing to do with her personally.

Do it, a satanic voice urged. Wake her up. Kiss her.

'I think we'd better go job-hunting,' he said in strangled tones, his eyes hopelessly enmeshed with hers.

'OK. But…about us staying on. Reconsider. A trial period. Please.'

Passion suffused her face. She looked radiant. And he could resist no longer. His mouth closed on hers and he groaned with hunger as she responded eagerly, inexpertly...but oh, so sweetly, the taste of her more succulent than the most exotic fruit, the pressure of her hand on his arm more welcome than he could ever have imagined.

Her hand slid to his neck. He drew her close, absorbing her into him, the needs of his mouth becoming more and more desperate as he sought to kiss life into every part of her.

To his astonishment, his neck was encircled in crushing arms, his head forced down till his mouth and thus his kisses became bruising. Laura had erupted. She was clamouring for him, moaning, crying, urging with a vehemence that startled and thrilled him to the core.

He lifted her onto him, her skirt riding up and her legs sliding around his waist. They clung in total abandon, not caring that anyone might drive by—although it was a rarely used road—oblivious to everything but the sensational release of long-held desires.

Her skin felt like velvet. Her hair tumbled over her forehead, silky and faintly perfumed of rosemary and he explored every inch of her face with impassioned delight.

He was weakening, kiss by kiss. Each wickedly innocent caress of her work-roughened hands aroused him more than any artful, silken finger. Laura was without artifice, her passion real and untaught.

That dazzled him, made his head spin with wonder. If he could have this glorious woman in his bed, he'd...

'Cassian!'

She had tensed. But he hadn't sated himself with her yet. So he continued to kiss her, to coax her now stubbornly closed mouth, sliding his tongue over it, enticing it open.

Except that it stayed resolutely closed, despite the sexual shudders which racked her body.

'Laura,' he murmured pleadingly.

'No!'

Oh, God, he thought, seeing her stricken face. She regrets what she's done. His arms fell away.

She looked down at her skirt, at the long lengths of slender tanned thigh which were making his loins liquid with their promise, and she gasped in horror then scrambled awkwardly away. With his reluctant help.

She turned her back, her face scarlet, eyes huge and glistening. Her skirt found its correct position. Her jacket was buttoned up, her hair hastily pressed smooth. And he saw with a wrench to his heart that her shoulders were shaking.

'Laura,' he ventured gently.

'No! Don't touch me! Don't come near me!' she squeaked.

'We just kissed,' he tried, playing it down.

Just! He'd seen stars. Been in heaven for a while. Dreamed impossible dreams.

Her head lifted and he dearly wanted to kiss the sweet nape of her neck.

'*You* might be used to grabbing women and—and—'

'Kissing them,' he supplied, seeing that she was struggling.

'Well,' she demanded, whirling around, all fire and passion again. 'Are you?'

How he wanted to take her in his arms again! That energy of hers needed an outlet—his, too.

'Not with such spectacular results,' he admitted, thinking how easily she'd aroused him.

She swallowed, as if horrified by his answer. And ran to the car. He didn't help her to get in. He didn't think she wanted to be touched.

He put his hands on the wall to steady himself because his legs seemed like water. His hands were shaking too.

Several deep breaths later, he'd come to the conclusion that he'd made things worse. Laura's hidden depths had come to the surface but he'd been almost drowned in the process. Of course he'd known from the start that Laura wasn't a run-of-the-mill woman. Whatever she felt, she felt fiercely.

So long as he realised that her uninhibited response hadn't been to him, *for* him, but was a reaction to her stifled emotions, he'd be all right. She would never want sex without strings. Whereas that was all he'd allow himself.

He gave her a moment to compose herself. Below, he saw that the deer had gone. It had found sanctuary. Perhaps, he mused, some people thrived better in their own small worlds.

The thought hit him like a sledgehammer. He could be wrong about extending Laura's field of vision, enlarging her horizons.

Yet now he'd kissed her, she could never remain at Thrushton—not if she wanted to stay out of his bed.

He muttered a low curse, went back to the car and settled himself in the driver's seat without comment.

'It never happened!' she whispered hoarsely.

He shot her a cynical look. If she thought he could ever forget that moment, she had another think coming.

The gears ground beneath his jerky grip. 'Let's concentrate on finding you employment, shall we?' he suggested, grinding the words out through his teeth as harshly as he'd ground the gears.

The beautiful scenery was lost on him. He kept blaming himself, trying to understand why he'd acted so precipitously. The desire for pleasure, he supposed. And, for a short time, what pleasure!

Once in Harrogate, he marched her off to a boutique. And, ignoring all her bad-tempered protests, coldly persuaded her that she'd get a job a hell of a lot faster if she wasn't wearing one of Aunt Enid's 'costumes'. If that's what it was.

Sulkily she saw the sense of what he was saying and insisted on paying him back out of her future wages. The assistant whisked Laura off and he lounged in an armchair, being plied with coffee and biscuits by a pretty redhead. Her legs weren't as good as Laura's. Nor her cheekbones.

'What do you think?' trilled the assistant smugly.

He turned his head and gulped like a teenage boy faced with a nude woman for the first time. Only this one was far better than nude. Dressed, she was absolutely breathtaking.

Finding his mouth was open, he closed it and summoned up as near-normal a voice as he could.

'Perfect.'

Laura's eyes had deepened to a startling sky-blue, enhanced by the soft navy dress. It skimmed her body but any connoisseur of women could see that she had a fabulous figure and the unbroken length of the sleeveless dress, grazing her collarbone and falling smoothly to just below the knee, made her look taller and more imposing than before. Helped by the elegant high heels and...surely new, sheer stockings.

As she moved in response to the assistant's instructions, he realised that Laura had incredible poise, her carriage as graceful as a model's.

'And there's a jacket to go with it that matches Modom's eyes,' the assistant crowed, bustling to put it on the increasingly astonished 'Modom'.

'Do you like it, Laura?' he asked dead-pan, entranced by her rapturous face.

She eyed him uncertainly. 'I do. I think it's gorgeous! But I don't think I'd be able to afford it—'

'Your...leaving present, then,' he suggested in clipped tones, finding the words ridiculously hard to say.

Her eyes widened in consternation. 'Leaving! Oh, yes. Leaving.' She gulped. The idea was obviously terrifying to her. He thought of the frightened deer. 'I—I don't know—'

'I do.' Feigning a frown, he stood up and handed over his credit card. 'I'm not hanging around any longer,' he said, with a good attempt at irritation. 'People to see. I've got an office to set up.'

'An office?' she repeated in amazement. *'You?'*

'For a colleague,' he growled. And realised he'd have to be careful if he was to keep his business a secret. 'Come on. That outfit is fine.'

And so with a little judicious bullying and much tutting at his watch, he rail-roaded her into accepting an expensive designer outfit, the shoes too, and a handbag which the assistant hastily found.

By the time they drove back later that day he'd leased a large Georgian building overlooking the green and had ordered the necessary office furniture and computer equipment. Sheila was due any time and he didn't want his charitable foundation to suffer any delays.

He wasn't the only one who'd had a successful day. Laura had four good job offers to consider. Success had wiped away her earlier distress and made her glow with pride. She looked utterly ravishing and he found it hard to keep his mind on the road.

This was a turning point for her, he thought. And wondered if she'd change, and become hard, efficient and slick.

Hopefully not. Since the incident in the restaurant when the waitress had flung banoffi pie over his arm, she'd mellowed towards him. That meant she had a soft heart. May it never harden. Wherever she went.

His stomach sucked in. There it was again. A pain. He didn't want her to go. Suddenly it was difficult to pump breath through his lungs. He felt as if he was panicking and set his mind to conquering his weak and wayward body.

'I'm in a total whirl!' she confessed as they bumped through Grassington's cobbled square. 'Which job do *you* think I ought to accept, Cassian?'

'It's your decision.'

His tone was abrupt enough to make her sink back into her seat and work out the pros and cons of each offer in silence.

Cassian couldn't understand why her success should bug him. What was he afraid of? He wanted her to extend her horizons and to become self-assured. Wanted her to have a better standard of living. Yet her imminent departure filled him with unease. No—be honest—misery. How could that be?

Appalled, his thoughts winged back to Jai again. It must be that he felt lonely. He and his son had never been apart for so long. That was it!

With a screech, he brought the car to a halt overlooking Thrushton village, the relief surging through him in waves.

'Got to ring Jai,' he explained, before leaping out.

Even in her bewildered state and with several job offers to consider, Laura noticed his urgency, the way he fumbled with the mobile attached to his belt and punched numbers with an almost frantic haste. He dearly loves his son, she thought soberly.

And the happiness that lit up his face when he spoke to Jai made her heart somersault. He didn't trouble to disguise how he felt. He looked thrilled, amazed, tender and amused, all in the space of a few moments.

He couldn't keep still, but strode about, gesticulating excitedly with his free arm, occasionally pushing a hand through his hair till it tumbled about in gypsy curls and made him look boyishly appealing.

If only she could be that free, that much at ease with Adam!

'Good news?' she queried, unable to hold back a smile. Cassian looked elated, his eyes sparkling like black diamonds.

'He's heading back!' Cassian leapt energetically into the car, beside himself with delight. 'Arriving later this week, depending on when he can get a flight. Isn't that fantastic?!'

His happiness was infectious and she found herself beaming. 'Wonderful,' she said huskily, wishing she could bring such a light to his eyes. 'We've both got something to celebrate.'

The light died a little. 'Yes. We have,' he said slowly.

And he suddenly jerked around, setting the car in motion again, his profile a confusing mix of pleasure and regret and anger.

Laura was puzzled. In fact he'd been odd ever since they'd met up after going their separate ways and she'd announced with pride how well she'd done in her interviews. His praise had been less generous than she'd expected and it seemed as if he was almost...sorry, yes, sorry, that she would soon be out in the world of commerce.

Had he hoped she'd fail? It didn't seem like Cassian. He was too big-hearted, too adamant that she should stop hiding herself away.

She glanced at him surreptitiously. He was frowning, his mouth grim. The tension in his hands would have been obvious to anyone. Perhaps his day hadn't been to his liking.

'What's wrong?' she asked softly.

His body contracted. He continued to glare at the road. 'Thinking.'

From the harshness of his tone, he didn't want to be disturbed. He shifted in his seat, drawing her attention to the flatness of his stomach, the stretch of soft moleskin over his thigh.

She drew in an involuntary breath before she knew what she was doing. He flicked her a sharp glance and the air seemed to thicken. She could feel her blood racing around her body, scalding her from within and she looked away, quickly.

Already she'd made a fool of herself. Perhaps that was what he was worrying about—wondering if she'd embarrass him in front of his son. She groaned inwardly. He must have been shaken by the way she'd responded to his kiss. Or had she made the first move? It had all been so sudden, so inevitable.

Whatever had happened to her? Had she unwittingly encouraged him? Had he—being acutely perceptive—read the signals she'd tried to hide…and acted on what he knew had been surging within her body?

She cringed, remembering with shame how abandoned she'd been, taking that kiss several stages too far. Cassian must have been appalled.

But… She bit her lip, frowning. Something had snapped inside her and she hadn't been able to stop herself. Her lack of control scared her. She needed to keep a tighter rein on herself.

So what about Cassian? Why had he taken up her unintentional invitation? Racking her brains, she remembered that they'd been talking about Jai. Heaven help her, she thought. She was a love-substitute. Cassian had wanted to be with his son—and he'd kissed her in an expression of his own loneliness.

Idiot! Stupid, arrogant dummy that she was! She stared into the window, seeing her own blurred reflection. A dull mouse; now dressed up in fabulous clothes, but clad in ghastly bottle-green yuk when they'd kissed.

She couldn't believe that she'd imagined he'd been interested in her. Would a man like Cassian ever be attracted to a homebody? Her eyes darkened. No. He'd go for the Bathsheba type: hot, passionate, simmering and unpredictable.

Her fingers touched her lips, every nerve in her body reliving the pressure of his mouth. It seemed that she had become hopelessly addicted to Cassian. Ever since he'd arrived there'd been a current of electricity linking them, setting her on fire.

Adam might hero-worship Cassian, she thought soberly, but so did she, after his behaviour today. His actions had proved him to be the kind of man she'd always admired. Thoughtful to others, courteous, easy company.

Lunch had been such fun. And he'd been so nice to the waitress, when the rather shaky-handed older woman had dropped the pudding onto his sleeve then burst into floods of tears.

To her amazement, he'd jumped up, put an arm around the woman's shoulders and drawn her aside, talking to her for a while and calming her down—totally ignoring the tight-lipped head waiter.

'Her husband's up for shoplifting,' he'd explained, when he finally returned to the table with profuse apologies for his absence. 'She thinks he might have Alzheimer's.'

'That's awful!' Laura had said, her eyes rounding. 'The head waiter was awfully mad—'

'Not any more, he's not.' Cassian accepted a substitute banoffi pie from a smiling waitress.

'Got you a big helping,' the young girl whispered. 'And thanks. That's my Mum you saved from the sack.'

'She'll be OK,' Cassian assured her quietly. 'I've arranged with the management that she can have time off to organise a decent defence—and a medical check for your father.'

For Laura, the rest of the meal had been spent in a haze of admiration. Now watching the houses of Thrushton loom nearer, Laura leaned back in her seat, her head filled with thoughts of Cassian and his kindness to people.

She knew that it hadn't been a show for her benefit. Kindness was ingrained in him. When she'd arrived early at their arranged meeting-point, she'd wandered through a department store and had seen Cassian unfolding a baby buggy while a young woman juggled child and shopping. Carefully he had tucked the toddler in, making it giggle while the mother had stowed away her laden bags. And they'd parted in smiles.

More important to Laura, a few moments later he'd

checked to see if she was in sight—not knowing she was following behind him—and made a point of going around the square to slip money into the hands of the young men who were begging there.

That had really touched her heart and melted any doubts she had about his values. It always upset her to see people reduced to such terrible indignities. Maybe some of them were 'fake'. But plenty were not. How did you ever know?

'Cassian…'

'Uh,' he grunted.

She searched for a diplomatic way to bring up the subject. 'Did you notice the beggars today?'

'Hmm.'

She waited for him to announce his generosity, but gradually realised that he wasn't the kind of person to boast about his good deeds.

'I never know what to do,' she confessed. 'Whether I'm condoning a drink or drug habit by giving them money, or if I'm actually helping them to buy a meal… What do you think?' she asked anxiously.

His mouth softened. She saw his shoulders drop and realised he'd been holding them in tension.

'There's no easy answer, no right or wrong. It's a question of conscience and judgement, isn't it?' he said gently. 'I like to make contact with them. I look into their eyes and talk to them and see if they're still on this planet and then decide. The method works whether you're in Yorkshire or Egypt, Russia or Columbia. However, I do give to the support groups—the hostels and so on. One day I hope that no one will be without a home. It's a basic human right.'

Laura considered this, remembering how he'd stopped to chat to each one, touching them, treating them like human beings instead of parasites or objects of loathing. He is compassionate, she thought shakily. And the knowledge brought her a quiet joy.

'It breaks my heart to think they have nowhere to be warm and safe,' she said in a small voice. 'I can't bear it. So I always give them money even though I don't know how to tell if they're on drugs or not.'

'But you're on the breadline yourself,' he said huskily.

Her eyes were big and dark with distress. 'And I have a home and a child who loves me! They have nothing, nobody! Imagine what that's like, Cassian!'

'I do,' he muttered bleakly. 'Often.'

She felt intensely disturbed by the depth of his caring. He was very special. Even as a child she'd known that. On several occasions she'd come upon him, secretly nursing an injured animal back to health. He had a way with animals; strong, gentle hands and a softly reassuring voice that encouraged trust. Dogs, cats, horses…they all fell under his spell.

Whenever he'd been with animals, there had always been a softening of the surly, angry expression he'd habitually shown to the world. And she remembered thinking how lovely it must be, to be tended with such devotion.

Laura hung her head. What must he think of her? That she was cheap and easy? She shuddered, wishing that she hadn't kissed him with such desperation. More than anything in the world, she wanted him to like and admire her. It baffled her why that should be.

Trying to unravel to mystery, she stole little glances at him, compelled to look, driven to gaze on him so often that he might have been her lover.

She stopped breathing for a moment. Lovers couldn't tear their eyes away from one another. *Love*… Could that explain the huge swelling sensation in her chest? The feeling that her mind had been electrified by a thousand volt charge? That she wanted to bury herself in him, to hold him and never let go?

Her muscles tensed. The extent of her passion was terrifying. Hot and trembling, she slid off her jacket after a complicated manoeuvre with the seat belt. And her senses screamed when Cassian's helping hand brushed her bare arm.

'I can manage!' she croaked.

'I'm sure you can,' he replied in a low and husky voice. 'But it would have been bad manners not to have come to your aid.'

'Sorry,' she muttered, feeling awful for snapping at him.

'It's OK. I imagine you're a bit preoccupied thinking about the jobs you've been offered,' he said generously. 'I'll leave you in peace.'

Peace! If only!

There was a brief touch of his hand on hers. She almost clasped it and gave it a fierce squeeze. Instead, she merely trembled.

Horrified, she realised that she was utterly infatuated with a man she hardly knew. A ridiculous situation.

Except...she felt as if she did know him. Perhaps she'd had these feelings before—when they were younger. She frowned. When he and Bathsheba had left Thrushton, had her sense of loss been so heart-wrenching because she'd believed herself to be in *love* with Cassian? Even at the age of fifteen?

And...had she unwittingly carried a torch for him all these years, perhaps even flinging herself at the salesman from Leeds because he too was dark and travelled about the country and had an air of independence like Cassian's?

Restless with the significance of her half-formed thoughts, she crossed her legs. And noticed his eyes lingering on the curve of her thigh. Her heart beat faster. Then she told herself that all men looked at legs. What she wanted, was a man who was interested in her. And that was highly unlikely where Cassian was concerned.

Anger set her eyes flashing and a fierce shaft of longing tightened her entire body. She wanted him with a ferocity of purpose that she'd never known before. Yet sheer common sense told her that at the best she'd be a woman to kiss and fondle. Nothing more. Nothing deep and lasting.

And in only a few days they would part, perhaps never to see one another again. She felt frantic at the thought, her heart cramping now that they were drawing up to the school to wait for Adam. It was all too late. Cassian would for ever remain a man she adored, his heart untouched.

Overcome with misery, she flung open the door and jumped out, her pulses thumping chaotically. It felt as if her life was disintegrating into tiny pieces. She knew at that moment that she had fallen headlong in love with Cassian.

It was a certain and instant knowledge. She'd always dreamed of being in love. But in her dreams her love had been returned and her lover had proposed marriage. She had imagined a Happy Ever After scenario but life wasn't like that. It was cruel and kicked you down whenever you got to your feet. One step forwards, two steps back.

Cassian had released her emotions; making her angry, afraid and defiant. With the opening of the flood gates, her passion for love had been also released from its prison of restraint, and she had joyfully emptied her heart to him.

But if you stuck your head above the parapet, there was a chance that you might get wounded. And wounded she was.

Choking back the sobs, she stood in forlorn silence, steeling herself to the fact that for the rest of her days she'd never find another man to match Cassian.

She loved him. Wanted him. But knew, with a sense of utter desolation, how hopeless her desires were.

CHAPTER EIGHT

LATER, she changed out of her finery and after a monosyllabic evening she sat pretending to read in the sitting room, while a silent and thoughtful Cassian sat opposite working on his laptop computer.

After school, he'd touched her heart still further by taking Adam for a walk then helping him with his homework and cooking supper. Steak and chips. Treacle sponge. Which Adam helped to make. Then treating Adam to a thrilling bed-time story, all off the top of his head.

Why did he have to be so flaming perfect?! she thought crossly. She was useless. OK, she conceded, maybe she'd landed those jobs and everyone had seemed more than anxious to have her on their staff... That was quite an achievement...

'You've been deep in thought for hours. I suppose you must have decided by now,' Cassian said quietly.

His eyes bored into her and she dropped her startled gaze in case he saw her naked adoration.

'Not yet. Toss up between the legal secretary and admissions clerk in the clinic,' she fudged, having hardly given them a thought at all.

'You must have been a brilliant interviewee.' His gaze held hers and she tried not to sink into a jellied heap but his voice was soft and dark as chocolate and persisted in rippling through her in silky rivers. 'Now do you believe me when I say you can do anything you want, if you want it badly enough?'

She smiled sadly. If only he knew what she really wanted! 'I hope that's true! But my references helped. People said some kind things about me.'

118

'They told the truth. Anyone can see how genuine you are; that you're honest and sincere and totally trustworthy,' he said quietly. 'It's plain that you'd be a conscientious and dedicated worker, and wouldn't contemplate giving anything less than one hundred per cent to your work.' He laughed at her open-mouthed amazement. 'I'm not kidding! Workers like you are few and far between. You have rare qualities, Laura.'

'Well, they only became apparent when I wore decent clothes,' she pointed out wryly, intoxicated by his words. Rare! She felt delirious from his praise.

'They got you noticed, I go along with that. Unfortunately people pay attention to appearances. But you won those job offers on your own merit so don't put yourself down. It's quite an achievement.'

She felt her breathing rate increase as hope spilled into her dulled brain. What had Cassian said? Something about applying yourself? If she wanted him to notice her, to respect her—and she did, oh, how she did!—then she needed time. Which she didn't have. Unless she very quickly made herself indispensable.

He wouldn't love her, she had to accept that. But could she settle for mutual friendship? Adam would benefit so much from Cassian's strength.

Living with the man she loved—and keeping her adoration a secret—would be agony. But it was better than never seeing him again, and for Adam's sake she must do everything she could to ensure that they remained in the house.

Looking at him from under her brows, seeing his long limbs draped easily over the armchair, she felt every inch of her body becoming fluid with adoration.

Quite subtly, so he wouldn't realise, she'd have to produce such gorgeous meals and make life here so incredibly comfortable, that he wouldn't want her to leave—whatever he'd said about being able to manage for himself.

He'd love being looked after—providing, she warned herself, she didn't ever curtail his freedom.

'You look sad,' she said gently. 'Are you thinking of Jai?'

His eyes flicked to hers and then darted away, his expression bleaker than ever.

'Something else.'

She had to bite her tongue to stop herself from asking 'what'. He'd tell her if he wanted to—and it seemed he didn't. It felt as if he'd slapped her around the face. It was all very fine, being Rare, but that didn't stop her from being excluded from Cassian's inner life.

She wanted to call out *Look at me, I'm here! Talk to me, confide in me!* But she couldn't bear the prospect of rejection. He didn't need her, he'd made that plain.

Her idea wouldn't work, she thought, her fragile confidence wavering. She'd never be able to hold back because she loved him so much. The sensible thing would be to close down. To shut out her feelings and become detached.

Her mouth shaped into a stubborn line. But she didn't want to! She wanted it all—the house, the job, Cassian. *Impossible.* Her eyes filled with tears.

Dimly she heard the trilling of a mobile phone and hid her wet face with her hand in case he noticed that she was being a wimp again.

'Cassian here,' he murmured into the phone and she flinched at his warm, rich tones. 'Hi, Sheila!' he said enthusiastically and she flinched again, this time because she wanted to be greeted with delight like that. 'How's things?'

There was a long pause during which Cassian's brows drew close together and his expression became concerned. Tactfully, Laura rose and slipped into the kitchen, wondering who Sheila might be that she could elicit such affection from him at first, and then reach into his heart to cause that look of deep consternation.

What a cloth-head she was! she thought grumpily, stoically drying her eyes and beginning to set out the breakfast things. Sheila was probably gorgeous. With ninety-four-inch legs, a degree in astro-physics and a background of extensive world travel. Oh, how could she ever have imagined that Cassian would give a damn about her—friend or otherwise?

And supposing he did, what then? They were too different for any relationship to blossom. She'd witnessed a similar disaster between her father and Bathsheba—and they'd been madly in love.

Little Miss Mouse, terrified of her own shadow, living on another planet to Cassian... The tears seeped inexorably upwards, clogging her throat.

'I'm going to bed.'

He'd spoken from the hall, his voice tight with strain. Scowling, she shot a quick look at him, surprised to see how defeated he looked.

Whatever Sheila had said, it had shattered him. Laura swallowed and furiously tried to stem the newly threatening tears. She wanted to affect him like that!

'Night,' she muttered, hoping he'd stay and tell her what troubled him.

He didn't move. It seemed as if all the stuffing had gone out of him. Her body ached with the yearning to run over and enclose him in a hug. But that wasn't her way.

'I'm going into Harrogate tomorrow,' he said flatly. 'Do you want a lift?'

So she wasn't to be his confidante. Bereft, Laura slammed the marmalade on the table.

'No. I'm shopping for Mr Walker.'

'What?'

Conscious that he was barely listening to her, she dealt out cutlery with unusual carelessness. Her life was one long round of fun, she didn't think.

'I told you about him. He's the one I shop for.'' Seeing he was still staring blankly into space, she felt compelled to let off steam. 'He's smelly and bad-tempered and he does nothing but moan and complain. I walk the two miles to Grassington, get everything he wants, walk the two miles back laden with bags, unload his shopping while he pretends I've got the wrong variety and have spent too much, and then I make him a cup of tea, settle him in his chair with a rug around him and we watch TV for an hour together. That's my excitement for the week. That's what I am,' she said with a sob. 'Miss Exciting. I really know how to live life, don't I? No doubt you're *riveted*!'

'Laura!' he cried, his brow furrowed in bewilderment. 'You're upset! Why—?'

'It doesn't matter!' she snapped, turning her back on him.

He pushed her around to face him again but she jerked her head to one side. Unfortunately her tears betrayed her and he gave a sigh then held her in his embrace.

'It does matter.'

'Only to me! And d-don't ask me if it's that time of the month,' she snuffled, 'because I'll scream!'

Cassian merely held her tighter. 'It's been an emotional few days for you,' he murmured in her ear. 'I would be surprised if you *weren't* on a roller-coaster.'

His hand lightly stroked her hair. It was a lovely sensation and she relaxed into him. But, to her dismay, he gently moved back.

'I didn't mean what I said about Mr Walker,' she mumbled. 'I do care. It's an awful life for him being confined to his house.'

'How long have you been doing all this for him?' Cassian asked quietly.

'I don't know. Ever since his wife died. I used to help her do her hair. She had arthritis in her fingers.'

Cassian drew in a long and hard breath. He seemed to be thinking about something and while he did, his finger lazily toyed with her fringe. She froze, afraid that any movement she made might make him stop.

'How badly do you want one of those jobs, Laura?' he asked hesitantly.

Blue eyes met brown. 'Desperately. I need a job to survive, you know that! How else can I afford champagne?' she jerked.

He smiled at her brave joke, took out his handkerchief and handed it to her. 'There's another job you might be interested in.'

'Sounds like an embarrassment of riches,' she commented, handing back the handkerchief.

Cassian pulled out a chair for her and sat nearby. Absently he rearranged the higgledy-piggledy cutlery in front of him and she waited, realising that he was searching for a way to tell her something.

'I...have a friend. A very good friend—'

'Sheila,' she hazarded.

How good, how friendly? her mind was demanding. Very? Bed friendly? Snuggle up together and exchange personal secrets kind of friendly?

He nodded. 'She runs a charitable organisation. Handing out money to deserving causes.'

Cassian's friend *and* with a wonderful job! Lucky Sheila.

'I envy her,' she said with a sigh.

Cassian felt his pulses race. She'd be perfect. Honest, reliable, conscientious and warm-hearted, with a love of humanity and a desire to help people in need. There was no one else he could turn to at such short notice. And yet common sense was telling him this would increase her involvement with him...

'She's had to give it up,' he said, pushing the words out before he got cold feet. The charity had to come first, whatever his doubts. 'She's flying to the States to look after her three nieces. Her sister and brother-in-law were killed in a car crash yesterday.'

'Cassian!' Laura cried in horror. 'That's terrible! The

poor little kiddies. Poor woman! Is someone with her? Do you need to go with her?'

She was holding his hand, giving him comfort. He could feel the firmness of her grip, the roughness of her work-worn fingers and somehow her concern was making his heart tighten as if it were in a vice.

'No. Her partner has gone with her. But…Laura, she's frantic about leaving the charity in a lurch. It's a small operation but it needs someone at its helm, someone who can be trusted not to misappropriate funds. People like that are hard to get—particularly at short notice.'

'I imagine so,' she said in concern.

Amazing, he thought. She had no idea of her qualities. Even now she had no idea that he was alluding to her. He took a deep breath, his passion for the charity overruling any personal wariness.

'Laura, I told her she could go immediately because I knew someone who could do the job.'

She smiled sadly. 'That's great. Sheila must have been relieved—'

'You,' he said. 'I thought of you at once.'

Her eyes widened, the spiky wet lashes blinking furiously. He wanted to kiss her. To take her to bed. He snatched away his hands and she looked upset at his rejection, her lush mouth trembling.

'You can't mean me! You can't be suggesting I take her place!'

He tried to keep his head—even if his body had decided to betray him and go off the rails. He cleared his throat and wondered if he had a cold coming.

'Who better? I've just set up an office for the charity in Harrogate—'

'Well, there you are. That lets me out. How do I get there? It's impossible, Cassian!'

His heartbeat quickened. She'd sounded deeply disappointed. 'You would commute, and get in whatever time you can. There aren't any rules attached to this job. Or I could drive you in sometimes. Then *you* will learn to drive. The charity will supply you with a car.'

Wistfully she said, 'And when Adam's ill?'

'No problem,' he said firmly. 'Much of the time—when he's ill, or if you have something special you need to do at home, you can operate from the house—'

'Sure. With no phone, no computer—'

'You're determined to find obstacles,' he said, amused. 'A phone line can be installed. This isn't the Sahara Desert. In the meantime you can use a mobile. The charity will set you up with everything you need, including a computer at home, plus anything else you need.'

'But…the cost—!'

'—would be a drop in the ocean. Particularly if the position goes to someone reliable and honest. There are a lot of sharks about. Money is a huge temptation and whoever runs this charity has carte blanche to sign cheques for massive amounts of cash. Appointing the right person is a real headache.'

'But…wouldn't you like the job?' she asked, puzzled.

'Me?' He hesitated. 'I'm…already employed.'

'Oh. I thought you must be looking for something. You've only just come from Morocco and you haven't exactly joined the 9—5 brigade,' she explained, looking excited at the prospect of landing the job.

'I…took time off.'

'What do you do?' she asked eagerly.

'Computer work. Laura, never mind me. What do you think?'

She chewed her lip. 'I don't know. It's a huge responsibility. I'm not sure I could do it—'

'You could! Listen. There's a fund. The income from its investments can be spent every year. Applications come in and the fund director—you—'

'Me? A fund director?' she asked, pink and beaming.

He laughed. 'That's what you'd be. And you'd sort through the applications, interview people from the charities applying, and write a cheque to those you think worthy, honest and with sound business plans. Simple. A matter of judgement. The salary would be at least double that of the jobs you've been offered—'

'Good grief! I couldn't take that much!' she protested. 'Not from a charity—'

'For heaven's sake, Laura!' he said impatiently. 'Value yourself! You'd earn it, I can assure you!'

'Well,' she said with a huge smile. 'I can always give the extra away, can't I?'

Typical. The people with least money were the most generous. He desperately wanted her to be financially secure.

'You'll do the job?' he asked, hardly daring to breathe.

'Don't I have to be interviewed? See a board of directors or something?' she asked with a frown.

'I told you. Sheila runs it. The directors are…kind of sleeping. She's left the matter of her replacement in my hands.'

'Why? What's your connection with the charity?'

'I contribute to it on a regular basis,' he said, omitting to tell her he was the only contributor.

She sighed. 'You are so generous. And, judging by the state of your four-wheel drive, you're not rolling in money.'

This wasn't the time to say he wasn't bothered about material goods and if a car moved, then he was happy with it.

'I get by,' he said blithely. 'Forget me. Say you'll do the job. It'll be a load off my mind and I know you'll be cracking at it.'

'I can't believe this! Yes, yes, I'd *love* to. Absolutely adore it!' she replied, her eyes shining brilliantly.

'Fantastic! Thank you!'

In sheer relief he caught her hands and grinned at her, completely bowled over by the delight on her face. Somehow they had moved closer and her lips were recklessly within reach. There was nothing in his lungs, not one breath. The very air seemed suspended as slowly he leaned towards her, a centimetre at a time so that she didn't take fright.

Her eyelids closed, her face lifted and he felt his heart soar as if he were being lifted on a thermal. Gently he placed a hand behind her head and let his lips touch hers. She quivered throughout the length of her body.

'Thanks,' he muttered.

The sweetness of her smile, the tenderness of her gaze, created mayhem in his head. This wasn't happening to him. Mustn't happen.

'I want to kiss you again,' he said with reckless disregard for sanity.

Solemn and painfully beautiful, she seemed to sink more deeply into his arms.

'It would be very unwise,' she said, encouragingly unsteady.

'Why?' he asked, his voice as thick and slow as a treacle.

'Because I'm going at the end of the week.'

His teeth clamped together. He had the impression that she was angling for an alteration to their arrangement. But if she stayed much longer than the next few days, he'd seduce her. And he must not do that. She was too precious, too vulnerable to handle a brief relationship. But a kiss or two would be all right.

'All the more reason to kiss you before you leave,' he murmured, pushing back the knowledge that he was deliberately deceiving himself.

She looked confused. 'Why do you want to kiss me?'

Cassian bit back an exclamation. He'd never been interrogated like this before! Trust Laura. He smiled at her, his finger running down the side of her soft cheek. She gave a little gasp and he knew she longed to let go. It would be good for her, he rationalised. A release of passion. Hell—it would be good for him too!

'Your mouth,' he husked recklessly, 'is soft and warm and far too near for me to ignore it. I like its taste. I like holding you in my arms...like your scent, the way your body yields, responds, matches mine for passion...'

She surrendered. With a series of little sighs, she let her lashes flutter down and allowed her lips to part. Gently he pulled her close. Felt her heart beating hard against his chest. The exquisite softness of her high, fast-heaving breasts and the tight hardness of her nipples, apparent even beneath the material of her shirt.

His head began to whirl. She wore no bra. It would take just a movement of his hand and...

He swallowed, checking himself ruthlessly. A kiss. Nothing more.

'You're so beautiful,' he breathed.

Her eyes snapped open, startlingly blue so close to his. 'What?'

The lightest of kisses. 'Beautiful.' Another one, delicate, whispering, tantalising every inch of his body with the effort of denial. 'Beautiful.'

'Oh!' she sighed in bliss.

He had no reason to be doing this except for sheer sensual pleasure. And pleasure it was. The smell of her, the feel of her hair beneath his fingers, the way she fitted him...

And he was using her. It wasn't fair. Wasn't right. Somehow he must extract himself from this situation without hurting her. Hell. Oh, hell, hell, hell.

Just a little more, a voice was telling him. A few kisses, a little more passion, the pressure of her mouth infinitely irresistible, the winding of her arms around his neck all that he could have wished for.

Against his chest her nipples were rock-hard now and

her mouth had become more daring, exploring his with a thoroughness that thrilled and unnerved him.

He had to get out of this, he thought hazily, crushing her closer. Willpower, that's all it took. All! When his entire body throbbed, his blood pounded so loudly in his ears that he couldn't have heard if she'd yelled, when his heart was in danger of going into cardiac arrest and his hunger had never, never been so desperate...

Somehow—who knew how?—he gentled their kisses, moving a fraction of an inch back each time. And wondered how he could do this when she was as hungry as he, willing, dizzy with desire...

'You,' he croaked, like a rusty hinge, 'are gorgeous.'

Her smile was intoxicating, lighting up her whole face. He couldn't leave it like this. She'd imagine this was the beginning of a courtship.

Cassian cursed himself for succumbing. It had been a mistake. Cruel.

He could hardly breathe. Certainly couldn't walk yet. He'd ache for hours.

'I know I shouldn't have done that,' he admitted hoarsely. 'But I can't say I'm sorry. I hope I haven't offended you...' A slight movement told him that she was moving away, both mentally and physically. 'I just had to kiss you,' he confessed with all honesty. 'An impulse. I was grateful—delighted that you'll take on the charity. And...you looked so lovely. Hope you understand. Forgive me?'

His eyes pleaded with her, begging her not to be hurt. Like an angel, she accepted his reasons, saw nothing evil in what he'd done. Perhaps because there had been no evil intended.

Her slow and seraphic smile mesmerised him. 'I understand.' Her eyes lowered, her mouth mischievous. 'It was a thrilling moment and it bowled me over,' she murmured. He tensed, every nerve in his body straining. And then he was stunned by his intense disappointment when she added demurely, 'To be offered such a wonderful, worthwhile job.'

'My gosh! You look terrible!' Laura said in amusement, when he staggered in from his run with Adam the next morning. 'Unshaven, bleary-eyed…what *have* you been doing?!'

'Bad night.'

'Why's that? Bed uncomfortable?' she asked innocently.

He was rescued by Adam. 'Race you to the shower!' Adam crowed, already leaping upstairs in his socks.

But Cassian didn't take up the challenge. He unpicked his laces, put his boots beside Adam's and slumped in a chair.

Now, mused Laura, usefully pouring him a black coffee, is this a man who's sexually frustrated and has spent the whole night trying to stop his hormones holding him to ransom?

She smiled a little smile of triumph. She did hope so! And she hugged her glee to herself that—for a brief time— he had found her mouth quite irresistible.

'I'm doing scrambled eggs. Shall I add some for you?' she asked serenely.

'Uh. Please.'

Grumpy and haggard and bemused. Looking at her legs again, slowly surveying her rear, her breasts… Her eyes gleamed. He was interested. He did like her. Respected her enough to offer her a high value job. That had meant a lot to her. And to top it all, she was both rare *and* gorgeous.

Her mirror that morning had agreed. After a deep, utterly contented sleep, she had woken to find someone else looking back at her—a confident, sparkling-eyed woman who oozed vitality.

She sang happily to herself, adding a few home-grown chives and tiny tomatoes from the garden to a buttered dish and slipping them in the oven to grill. For the first time, she really believed that she could achieve her life-long dream. Her voice strengthened, bursting with joy, the notes clear and true, every inch of her body surrendering to happiness.

Cassian slowly stumbled out of the kitchen, his tread heavy and laboured on the stairs. Her singing grew louder, more ecstatic.

It took Mr Walker only a short time, however, to bring her down to earth again. Morose and uncommunicative, Cassian had acted as chauffeur so that she could do Mr Walker's shopping and then be free to investigate the office in Harrogate.

'I hope you don't mind,' she said hesitantly, when the old man opened the door, 'but I've brought—'

'Cassian!' Mr Walker cried in delight. 'Cassian!' he added with soft affection.

Laura was open-mouthed when Cassian strode forwards and gave Mr Walker a gentle bear hug.

'Tom,' he said fondly. 'You old reprobate! Sitting around like Lord Muck, and letting a tame dolly bird do all your shopping...you ought to be ashamed of yourself!' he teased.

'Man's gotta get what pleasures he can at my age,' chuckled the old man. 'Sight of those legs of Laura's sets me up for the whole day!'

Blushing, the astonished Laura went into the tiny kitchen and began to unpack the groceries, oddly pleased that there was some kind of bond between the two men.

'You know each other, then,' she commented when they both appeared, Cassian with his arm around Mr Walker's frail, shawl-wrapped shoulders.

'Go a long way back.' The old man eased himself painfully into the rocking chair by the iron stove. 'Cassian used to come here when he was a lad. We went fishing together. My Doris lent him books. Great reader, my Doris.

Devoured encyclopaedias, Cassian did… Hang on a minute, lass!' he protested. 'That's not proper ham!'

'It's what you always have,' she said calmly, conscious of Cassian, dark-eyed and silent in the corner.

Mr Walker muttered under his breath, picking over his supplies for the week. 'I've told you I don't like big oranges. And those sprouts look manky. Useless woman,' he goaded, picking up the bill and glaring at it. 'You bring me rubbish and there's twopence more on the bill?' he snapped.

'I know,' she said with a sigh. 'I'm awfully sorry—'

'You're on the wrong track,' Cassian said to Tom Walker, suddenly alert. 'Try attacking something she cares about.'

Mr Walker's watery eyes narrowed. She thought there was the suspicion of a smile on his sour face before he said in contempt,

'Her? She's a waste of space. And her kid's as dopey—'

'Don't you dare talk about my son like that!' she flared, her eyes scorching with anger. 'I can take your bad temper and your ingratitude because I feel sorry for you but Adam's off limits! *Do you understand?*' she yelled, banging the table so hard that the vegetables jumped in shock and rolled to the floor.

To her astonishment, Mr Walker grinned so hard that his toothless gums showed. Cassian was laughing.

'Now *that's* your mother talking!' cackled Mr Walker.

She froze. *'What?'* she ground out furiously.

'I've bin trying for years to get you angry, lass!' he wheezed, tears of laughter running down his face. 'Wanted to see if you'd got your ma's fire in your belly. Almost gave up. All you did was apologise like you was made of milk and water. But you're like her all right,' he said more gently. 'More life in her than most. Lovely woman. Miss her, something chronic, I do.'

She sat down, her legs weak. 'You…you devious, mean

old man!' she said shakily but she couldn't hide her pleasure. 'Am I…am I really like her?'

'Spitting image. Beautiful, she was. Had a temper on her, though.'

'Tell me!' she begged. 'I know nothing about her, nothing! Please! Tell me the circumstances surrounding my birth. Everything.'

'Well, I'm blowed. I thought you knew *that*. Well, let's see. I know George Morris didn't treat her right. Bullied her. Any fool could see how unhappy she was and that she longed to be loved proper, like. Anyroad, she fell headlong in love with the American who took over Killington Manor, down the dale just beyond Little Sturton, where I worked as a groom. Found she was pregnant—and George hadn't touched her for over a year. But, proud devil that he was, he wouldn't agree to a divorce so she tried her level best to settle back into her marriage. Doomed, it was, though.'

'My…father was…American?' she said faintly.

'S'right. Nice chap,' said Mr Walker. 'Jolly sort—'

'More!' she begged. 'I want to know more!'

'More, eh? He was tall, dark, smiling eyes, if you know what I mean. Easy-going hospitable type. Publisher. Crazy about your mother, but then few could resist her lovely nature.'

'All this time I've known you…why…*why* didn't you tell me all this?' she wailed.

'Thought you knew bits and pieces, lass. When I realised you didn't have much of a clue, I thought I'd better keep my trap shut. Not my business to interfere. Wasn't sure you were tough enough to hear the truth.'

'They didn't speak about her mother,' Cassian explained. 'It was a taboo subject.'

'But…*you* knew!' she stormed at him.

'Yes,' he admitted. 'But until you told me a few days ago that Thrushton Hall was the only link you had with your mother, it had never occurred to me that they hadn't told you the basic facts, or that you had no tangible memories of her—photos, possessions…I still can't believe they'd do that to you! Poor Laura. This is outrageous…'

Clearly upset, he put his arm around her shoulders. Gratefully she leaned into him, touched by his anger on her behalf. She felt nothing but contempt for George and Enid's refusal to explain her background.

'But why did my…' She checked herself. Never again would she call George Morris 'father'. 'Why did George get custody?'

'Because everyone thought you were his child,' Cassian said gently.

Laura felt a sickening sensation clutch at her stomach.

'Didn't my *real* father claim me? She must have gone to him, surely? Didn't they run away together? Didn't they want me?' she asked miserably.

The old man looked uncertainly at Cassian, who brought her close to him as if protecting her.

'She can deal with it,' he said in low, quiet tones.

Laura's hopes collapsed. 'Oh, no!' she groaned. 'You're not telling me they're…*dead*?'

Mr Walker's eyes were gentle, his expression loving and full of regret.

'Both of them, lass. Her and the American. It was filthy weather. Tractor came out of a field and into the Harrogate road and killed them outright two weeks after you were born. He was bringing you and your mother back to Killington Manor to live with him. George Morris brought you up as his daughter and only a few of us knew the truth.'

A sob escaped her. She had been so close to having a truly loving home. And her mother had been denied the happiness she'd hoped for.

It was unbelievably sad. Laura gave a moan and flung her arms around Cassian's waist for solace.

'They never said!' she mumbled. 'All these years I privately feared that she'd rejected me, *abandoned* me—led on by heavy hints from George and Enid. Oh, that was cruel, Cassian, cruel!'

She burst into floods of tears. There were years of weeping inside her but the two men just held her and patted her and waited while she mourned the parents she'd never known.

Dimly she became aware that the men had been talking for a while.

'...say goodbye properly. Got a map, Tom?' she heard Cassian ask quietly.

A map! She felt indignant but kept her head buried in his middle hearing the rustle of paper. Cassian wanted to look at a route to somewhere, when she...

'Just there,' said Tom Walker. 'That little lane...'

'And the gate?' Cassian asked softly.

Her heart turned over. Guilt swept through her as she realised what Cassian was doing. Bless him, she thought. Bless him.

'Take me there!' She pleaded, choking and hoarse, the words disappearing into his soft shirt.

His hand was infinitely gentle on the silk of her hair. 'Come,' he muttered, his voice cracking. 'We'll pick some flowers from the garden. We can make a lovely bunch for your mother from the roses, agastache, helenium, salvia...'

'And if you come round one day, both of you,' said Mr Walker kindly, 'we can have tea and talk about your parents, if you'd like. I'm very fond of you, pet,' he added. 'You're like a dear daughter to me.'

'I'd like,' she said in a small voice. And kissed him. Suddenly she felt overcome with emotion and her arms tightened about the skeletal frame and she held him tight. 'See you soon,' she whispered.

He nodded, his eyes filled with tears. 'Say hello to her from me,' he rasped. 'Good friend. Warm heart. Like you. I promised her, at her funeral, that I'd keep an eye on you. She'd be proud of you, Laura.'

She couldn't speak for emotion. In a blur she saw Cassian clasp Tom Walker's hand, an unspoken message of affection exchanging between them.

'Old times,' Cassian said softly. 'We have a lot of catching up to do, Tom. Till then.'

Gently he ushered Laura out of the door. His arm was around her as they walked along the street to the manor house, guiding her feet, holding her firmly when she stumbled because the tears were obliterating her vision.

But he stood back while she picked the flowers, knowing that this was something she needed to do on her own. These were her gift to her mother.

And even though he waited a yard or so away, his tenderness enfolded her, protecting her like a supporting blanket. Without him she would have broken down. With him, she felt she could cope.

'How did you know that Mr Walker was goading me?' she asked in a pitifully little voice.

'Partly because he's a kind man and I could see from his eyes that his heart wasn't in what he was doing, and partly because I'd been trying to do the same.'

Her eyes widened and accused him. 'Provoke me, you mean?'

'Sort of,' he confessed. 'When you talked about Adam, I could see that underneath you were a woman of deep passions and fierce beliefs. For your sake, Laura,' he said gently, 'I wanted you to find your guts before you were thrust into the world. It's a wonderful and exciting place. I wanted you to enjoy it.'

She heaved a sigh. The end of the week was a long way away at the moment.

'I'm finding my emotions all too easily,' she said jerkily. 'You're stripping away all my barriers and I'm left raw and open and hurt!'

His eyes softened. 'But you're in touch with your heart.'

'It's a painful process,' she muttered.

'There's joy too,' he promised.

'Really?' she mumbled, her face wan.

Because she wasn't sure she believed him. A chill went through her. Passion, she thought, gripped in an icy fear. Was it truly worth the anguish that came with it?

CHAPTER NINE

IT WAS a fifteen minute drive to the accident spot. For the rest of her life she would remember the powerful musky perfume of the roses in the confines of the car, and the comfort of Cassian's reassuring hand on hers when they finally reached the place Mr Walker had described.

'Wait. I'll help you out,' Cassian offered.

So kind and tender. He seemed to know instinctively what to do, what to say, when to be silent.

Her pulses drummed. Her face was almost as white as the mallow flowers in her hands. Shakily she clambered down and lifted her head up high.

Alone, she walked to the farm gate, thinking only of her mother's tragic death and of the American man who had been her mother's lover. Her father. A man she would have loved if she'd known him. What had he been like? She didn't know. She couldn't visualise him.

Her eyes filled with tears again. It was awful, not knowing either of her parents. She bit her lip. For most of her life she'd unwittingly lived a lie created by George and Enid Morris.

Fervently she asked for her mother's forgiveness for doubting her. Laura had been swayed by the endless false-hoods and half-truths. Cheated of her past, deceived, and twisted so that she fitted into a mould of George Morris's choosing.

She could have been lively and passionate and beautiful, given the chance. She might have been the kind of woman who flung her arms around people, like Sue, and breezed through life without hang-ups.

Her heritage had been taken away from her. And now she didn't know what kind of person she was.

And yet despite her sadness, Laura felt the inexorable beauty of her surroundings seeping into her. The lane ran along a valley, eroded long ago by the meltwater from an ice sheet. Close by were the remains of a medieval village, abandoned in the plague. Buttercups made the valley golden in the September sun. In early summer, she mused, the meadows would be a riot of colour, red clover, pignut and cranesbill vying with the buttercups and marguerites.

The high drystone walls were thick with lichen and moss and she reached out to touch the soft green mat covering the massive limestone rocks. Here in this lovely valley she could imagine her mother's spirit. Here she could find solace and comfort.

'I love you, Mum,' she husked, an overwhelmingly powerful emotion deepening her voice and making it shake. She didn't find it odd to be standing in a country lane and talking aloud. It seemed right and natural and it unburdened her heart. She took a deep breath and continued passionately. 'I wish I'd known you and Father! Wish I'd lived with you! Oh, I wanted that so badly. We could have been happy, the three of us.'

Again she thought how different she might have been. More open, less guarded, more ready to laugh and cry. Less afraid to show her love. To be loved.

Her heart aching, a hard, painful lump in her throat, she strewed the flowers about the lane and bowed her head while goldfinches chattered sweetly nearby.

'I'll make you really proud of me,' she promised. 'I won't let myself become like Aunt Enid: mean and caustic, critical and unfulfilled. I will go for happiness...follow my heart. I will hug people if I feel the urge. I won't let my life go to waste, I won't!' she sobbed. 'And I'll help Adam to be strong, now I know how. You'd love him, Mum, Dad...'

She couldn't speak for crying. It felt as if her heart was full of love and sorrow at the same time. It seemed to be expanding from where it had been lying cramped and afraid in her chest. Now it beat with her mother's blood, her father's passion. And she felt whole at last.

She shivered and a moment later she started when she felt a jacket being gently draped about her shoulders.

'You're cold. You've been here a long time,' Cassian said huskily.

Her forlorn, tear-washed face lifted to his, instinctively seeking something from him.

'Hold me,' she pleaded.

With a mutter of concern, he took her in his arms and let her squeeze him as hard as she could. After a moment the violent tensions in her muscles eased and she sagged against him.

'They...sound as if...they were lovely people,' she sniffed jaggedly.

'And you are their child. Remember that. You are like them,' he answered, stroking her back.

'That's a n-nice thing to s-say.'

'Just the truth,' he breathed into her hair. 'Perhaps now you can be yourself. Be free.'

The thought comforted her. She could start again. Despite her anguish, she felt an uplifting feeling. 'Can we walk?' she mumbled.

'Whatever you like, whatever you need. Hold my hand, you're shaking,' he said softly.

With infinite care, he helped her over a ladder stile and into the field beyond. For a long time they strolled quietly with just the plaintive cry of the lapwings eerily breaking the silence.

They found a sheltered spot to sit. They gazed at the view from high above the strip lynchets, the terraced fields which had been hacked out of the hillside centuries ago, even long before the Black Death in the fourteenth century which must have parted so many loved ones.

The wind ruffled her hair and brought sharp colour to her cheeks. This was her beloved Yorkshire. The place where her mother and father had fallen in love and where they had died. And she would do anything to stay here for the rest of her days on earth.

His hand gripped hers tightly. His eyes were like liquid velvet and she felt more cherished than she had in the whole of her life.

And for no reason at all, her tears suddenly cascaded down her face in torrents.

'Laura, Laura!' he whispered, turning her to him.

His lips touched her cheekbone then travelled around her face stopping each tear that fell. She felt a desperate need to be comforted by him, to lose herself in his kisses.

Lifting her mouth, she caught his face between her hands and let her eyes do the asking.

'Kiss me properly,' she moaned.

Cassian stared helplessly. 'Don't mistake what you're feeling,' he rasped. 'You're—'

'I want to be kissed!' she insisted.

'Because you want to be comforted.' He sounded bitter and his teeth were clenched together hard. 'I'll hold you, but I won't do more—'

'Why?' she demanded, shuddering with intense fervour.

'You'd regret it later, when you're not so distraught—'

'I won't!' she whispered, adoring his mouth, the smoothness of his face beneath her fingers.

Desperate to lose herself in his lovemaking, she explored his mouth with a thoroughness that shook her. She laced her fingers through his hair, subtly trapping him, her body pressing hard against his.

It was wonderful when he responded, a groan preceding his impassioned surrender to her wiles. They couldn't get enough of each other, their hands clutching, roaming, invading…

She was caught up in the intensity of her feelings, her mind closed to all but the sensations surging through her frantic body, everything centred on the need to touch Cassian, to be touched…loved, not to miss a moment of life and happiness.

If she loved him, and she did, she wasn't going to waste time being coy. She'd take what she wanted, be what she wanted, obey the call for love that was overriding everything else in her mind and body.

She was crying and gasping, moaning and panting just like him. His hands wove magic spells in her body, every part of her seemingly set alight by his caress.

Each breast quivered, bloomed, tightened unbearably from the gently erotic movement of his questing fingers. The heat of his loins burned into her till she thought she must have reached melting point.

At some time they must have sunk back to the ground. Here, her arms demanded, legs slithered urgently, pelvis arched in throbbing hunger. She was dimly aware that her mouth knew now every inch of his face and throat, the hard satin of his chest, the hollows of his stomach.

Her clothes had largely disappeared, like his, though when he—or she—had removed them she couldn't have said. Her desperation matched his. Her desire to kiss and touch every inch of him was echoed by his unstoppable ravishment.

The surface of her skin felt hot and tingling as if it had been electrified. Each of Cassian's fierce, impetuous kisses stirred her very blood and pushed her to a more intense state of excitement.

'I can't bear it!' she whispered, seeking without success to undo his belt.

She felt him kick away her skirt, and, unhampered, she wound her legs about him so that she could drive her pelvis

harder into his body and ease some of the terrible need
within her.

His mouth swooped on hers, enclosing, warm and almost
frantic in its kisses. The pressure of his hand cupped around
the cleft between her legs and even through her small cotton briefs she could feel the heat, the glorious movement
of the heel of his hand. And then, with a wriggle, she had
ensured he touched her flesh.

'Ohhhhh…'

'Laura!' he croaked.

Her loving hand stroked his face, her eyes anxiously encouraging him.

'Please,' she whispered.

'I—this is not right…I—'

'I need you, Cassian!' she rasped. And touched him.

His eyes closed as he did battle with himself. Gently she
moved her hand, feeling the leap of power beneath her
fingers.

'No, no, no…' he moaned.

'You told me to live!' she whispered, slipping her tongue
between his lips. 'I am living. This is what I want. Love
me. *Love me!*' she moaned into his mouth.

She mimicked the act of making love, her own body so
aroused that she wondered how it could still obey her. But
then she was operating on instinct. And love.

Cassian tore his mouth away, his face strained. 'But afterwards—'

'Forget afterwards. This is now,' she said fiercely.

She took his hand, let his fingers meet the throbbing bud
between her legs and uttered a long, low moan of pleasure.
This was what she'd longed for. Physical release with the
man she loved.

The ecstasy in her body was nothing to the joy in her
head, her heart and her soul. Cassian would possess her.
She would know him and he would know her. If she died
tomorrow, she would have been a part of him.

He could feel her mouth bruising his. Heard the little gasps and moans, the outrush of her sweet breath as he rhythmically caressed her. The beauty of her body had stunned him.

The soft mounds of her breasts met his mouth and her nipples rose obediently to his gentle suckling as she bucked and shuddered beneath his arousing fingers.

Too far…he'd gone too far to step back. It terrified him, this sensation of losing total control, of being unable to master his passion. What had she woken in him? he thought, slipping further from reality, mesmerised by the alluring Laura, by her sublime eyes, her hungry mouth and fabulous, irresistible body.

Quite helpless, driven by something he didn't understand, he clawed at his belt and managed by accident rather than luck to undo it. In a moment they were both naked. Flesh to flesh. He trembled, intoxicated by the sensation.

'Are…' He tried again, swallowing back the choking emotion. Pausing only briefly to wonder what was happening to him. 'Are…you…sure?'

There was a beauty about her face, as it swam beneath him, that made his heart turn over. Her dreamy smile dazzled him, leaving him blind.

'Sure,' she breathed. 'More sure than I've ever been.'

A volcano was threatening to burst inside him but he caressed her gently, taking his time till her pleas were so loud and insistent that he knew she was more than ready.

A sense of wonder flooded his mind as he gently eased into her, their bodies sliding so naturally together that they had surely been made for one another.

And then his world exploded. All he knew was that something unbelievable was occurring, a scattering of his senses and a fierce high voltage arousal of every cell in his body.

A storm erupted in his head. Sweet torment surrounded every nerve, tugging and caressing, thrilling and teasing

until he didn't know where he was or what he was doing…only that this was lovemaking at its most awe-
inspiring and this was love with Laura and he never wanted
it to end…

The pounding in his ears blotted out her cries—or were
they his?—and his body erupted in a wild release of joy
and pleasure. Warmth flooded him. And a deep, intense
peace.

Her hands moved lazily over his back. Still in a state of
disbelief, she smiled to herself. This was why people became obsessed with one another, then! Her heart was soaring. As free as that bird she could see high up in the sky…a
lark, surely?

Now she fully understood her mother. When you found
true love and a passion that matched your own, it was hard
to deny. She was so happy. Madly, hugely, ferociously!

'Cassian,' she whispered into his ear.

'Mmm.'

She wound her arms around his neck. He lifted his head
which had been buried in her neck and looked at her as if
he was drunk. Her eyes shone, her adoration plain for him
to see.

'Is it…always like that!' she asked, not sure if she could
physically bear such sweet torment too often.

He kissed her soft mouth. 'Hardly ever,' he said wryly.
'What did you do, Laura? Drug me?'

She laughed and kissed him back. No. She'd only loved
him. Given him everything. 'Good, was I?' she asked
smugly.

His eyes darkened till they were like glittering black
onyx.

'Sensational,' he growled.

She was going under again; the desire flaring up from
the igniting of his body moving over hers. Her eyes closed,
all the better to enjoy the unbearably slow, rhythmical

strokes inside her and the delicious sensations chasing on and in and through each part of her.

'Cassian,' she murmured and slithered sensually against him, provoking him with her body, biting him, enjoying the tension of his muscles under her sensitive hands.

'Sweet Laura,' he said hoarsely, kissing her throat.

The little stabs of energy began to thrust at her and she let them take her over, revelling that she could abandon herself without fear. She trusted Cassian. And so she could dare to behave freely.

''Swunnerful,' she slurred, clinging to him.

He flipped her over, hauled her up, cupped her heavy breasts in awe and flicked his tongue over each engorged nipple. Then his hands pressed on her hips till she felt the deepest, most incredible completion of herself.

And she began to move, watching his face, seeing the infinite pleasure she could give him, aroused beyond belief by the blissful expression on his beloved face.

The climax came hot and fast, rushing up to take her unawares. It shot her up to a pinnacle of sensation and then slowly released her, till she found herself safe and warm in the welcome of Cassian's strong arms.

It was a while before he dressed her. Tired and bemused, she let him do so, offering a leg or an arm like a docile child. She was far to 'high' to do anything for herself.

This was emotion—and she loved it, she mused, as his handsome face contorted with a frown while he tried to manoeuvre her skirt over her hips. With a sigh, she lifted her pelvis. Their eyes locked. Hot passion spilled between them, Cassian kissed her, hard.

'I can't leave you alone!' he muttered.

'Good,' she crowed.

'No, it's not...'

'Why?' She lifted her arms over head, intentionally provocative.

'Please, Laura!' he groaned. 'We have to get back. Harrogate's off, but you'll need to be home for Adam.'

'Is it that late?' she said in stunned surprise.

'We seem to have missed lunch,' he said, amused.

'No, we didn't!' she laughed and he kissed her tenderly.

In a daze they stumbled back to the car. Laura paused for a moment in the lane, trying to visualise her mother as someone alive and vital and very much in love, very loved, chattering happily as her lover drove her and their baby to Killington Manor.

Her mother would have been happy. As happy as she, Laura, was now. A long sigh escaped her parted lips. Today she had found great sorrow and great joy. This, she vowed, would be a relationship that would survive.

'Do you want to be alone?' Cassian asked with typical tact.

They were holding hands and she gave his a quick squeeze of thanks.

'No.' She didn't ever want to be alone again. 'Thank you for bringing me here. Let's go home,' she said, deeply content.

'Tom has told me where your parents' graves are,' Cassian said quietly. 'I'll take you there. And I think Adam should come too.'

She was overcome with gratitude. 'Thank you,' she said again.

They met Adam from school and took him to the small churchyard in a small village beyond Killington Manor, close to the river. Gently Laura told him about his grandparents while Cassian checked the gravestones.

'Here,' he said, holding out his hands to them.

Laura's heart pounded. She swallowed and gripped Adam's small hand in hers. Cassian enfolded them both in his arms, shepherding them towards a small, nondescript stone above an untended grave.

'I can't read it!' she mumbled, her eyes awash.

'It says…"Here lie Jack Eden and Diana Morris",' Cassian said huskily. 'Then there are the dates…and below it is written; "tragically taken from this world but together in the next." Tom Walker had that stone put up,' he told Laura. 'There was a scandal because George and Enid wouldn't pay for the funeral but those who worked at Killington had a whip-round for it. The house was sold and incorporated into your father's estate. Since your father hadn't changed his will, everything went to some distant cousin in New York. Tom was upset that you had nothing. He has watched over you ever since.'

'People are so kind!' she said shakily. 'I don't mind about the money. I have so much, compared with others.'

'Don't cry, Mum!' begged Adam.

She hugged him hard. 'I'm sad and I'm happy. Do you understand, darling?'

His big blue eyes softened. 'Yes, I do, Mum. I'm sorry they're dead. I'd have liked grandparents. But I'm glad they didn't abandon you.' His skinny arms wrapped tightly around her. 'I love you, Mum,' he said fiercely. 'Everything'll be all right now.'

She smiled and met Cassian's infinitely tender eyes. 'Yes,' she breathed, kissing her son's fair head. 'I think it will.'

That evening, when supper and the run and homework were all dealt with, all three of them sat on the sofa together and talked. And when Adam had gone sleepily up to bed, she curled up in Cassian's arms watching a documentary on TV.

Occasionally he kissed her. But most of the time it was enough that they were close. He was wonderful, she thought happily. And he seemed compelled to touch her. Not sexually, but just small touches; a stroke of her hand, the brush of his fingers down the side of her cheek, the increased pressure of his arm around her waist for no particular reason.

In her book, that meant one thing. Whether he knew it or not, he was rapidly finding he couldn't do without her. She hoped that was true. All her hopes were pinned on that fact.

'I wish I could take you to bed,' he growled in her ear.

'Well, you can't,' she said, secretly delighted with his regret.

'I know. It's torture. I want to fall asleep with you in my arms, to wake and find you beside me.'

'Me, too!' she whispered, overjoyed that he wanted her presence as much as she wanted his.

'I'll take you to the office tomorrow,' he rasped. 'And I will make love to you as you've never known it before.' Abruptly he stood up. 'I must go now, Laura,' he said, desperately running his hands through his hair. 'See you in the morning.'

She couldn't believe it. He needed her very badly. And everything he said suggested that it wasn't just sex but something deeper. Hopefully more lasting.

Walking on air, she floated off to bed and fell into a contented sleep the moment her head touched the pillow.

CHAPTER TEN

'THE blue or the green?' she asked the next morning in the Harrogate office, waving silky scraps of froth, which were masquerading as panties.

'Breen. Glue...Laura!' groaned Cassian, when she gurgled in delight at his confusion. 'My brain doesn't work when you prance around like that.'

'Like what?' She pranced. Tried a little modified lap dancing.

Naked and menacing, Cassian growled alarmingly and came straight for her. She squealed and dashed around the buttonback sofa. But not too fast.

'Temptress,' he muttered, catching her and covering her with kisses.

He bent her backwards, Silent Picture Style, and she fluttered her lashes at him, making Silent Picture Faces at him.

'I think I'm going to like coming here,' she said smugly.

'You won't get sex every time, you know,' Cassian said with a grin.

'Shame! I suppose I'd better get dressed.' Her eyes sparkled, a deep and intense blue. 'Have another glass of celebratory champagne while I shower. Then I'm handing out money to people who deserve it,' she said happily.

'You think you have everything you need?' he enquired.

She paused, her eyes glazing over. He was gorgeous. Standing there absolutely naked, totally masculine and unbelievably thoughtful. His hair was tousled, eyes drugged whenever he looked at her, body...quite breathtakingly beautiful. What more could a woman want?

Yes. She had everything.

'It's all perfect,' she said with a sigh.

Glowing with love, she cast her eyes about her. The offices were gorgeous too. High ceilinged and with the lovely proportions of a typical Georgian mansion, they had been tastefully decorated and fitted out so that the overall effect was that of a comfortable high class home rather than a business empire.

They were in the interview room, having made the best use of the deep cream carpet she could ever have imagined. Their clothes were strewn everywhere. The results of their shopping—wicked and seductive lingerie and two more outfits for her, plus clothes for Adam and small decorative touches to make the office more friendly—were heaped on the comfortable sofas.

When she was ready, she was to employ someone to open mail and to deal with her correspondence. Until then, she could settle in at her own pace. It seemed too good to be true. But it was real enough. She'd seen the letters asking for help and was anxious to get started.

'Thank you for this chance,' she said, beaming with pleasure.

'Thank *you*. You'll be wonderful,' he answered huskily.

Blowing Cassian a shy kiss, she wandered into the huge marble bathroom and turned on the shower. She was to work for a while and Cassian would help her with the mail, then they were going out to lunch.

When they arrived back at Thrushton Hall, Cassian and Adam would go out for their run and then on their return the house would be filled with the sound of laughter and noise and fabulous music, just as it had been last night.

She smiled, thrilled with the change in Adam. He *was* more confident, more feisty. And she'd listened to the sound of Cassian's voice in the house upstairs as he'd read some exciting story to her son, and her heart had seemed fit to burst with happiness.

A fabulous meal was in order tonight, she thought, mentally going through the recipe she'd chosen. With a month's advance salary in the bank, she'd felt able to buy something special to strengthen her plan to be totally indispensable to Cassian.

Fillet of beef rolled in herbs and porcini, wrapped in prosciutto. Her mouth watered as she stepped out and dried herself. Chocolate pots and sharp lemon wedges. Her eyes lit up. He'd adore it, while she'd adore cooking for the men she loved. And tomorrow there'd be succulent chicken in wine sauce followed by bread and butter pudding laced with whisky. Heaven.

'Champagne.' Cassian handed her a glass and switched on the shower for himself.

'To the future. Happiness for all,' she said, lifting the elegant flute, confident now that he'd want her to stay.

He smiled fondly. 'The future. Happiness.'

In a daze of delight she eased on her elegantly fitting Jackie-O dress and then, with great pride she settled at her huge desk with its view across the leafy park.

Her mind was teeming with thoughts of the future— Cassian falling in love with her, the two of them and their sons living happily together, perhaps a child of their own...

The shower door banged in the background and she hastily put her dreams on hold and began to tackle the post.

'So many people needing help!' she marvelled, when Cassian came in.

He grabbed a stack of letters and began slitting them. 'I know. It can be heartbreaking. But we...I mean, the charity can make a difference to some. I suggest you make a rough selection of "Good grief no's" and "so-so's" and "yes, desperate's", and I'll keep them coming.'

Her 'yes, desperate' pile was unnervingly large when they'd finished opening all the letters.

'Supposing I give out all the money in two months and there's none left?' she said anxiously.

'Then you have ten months of twiddling your thumbs,' he said, grinning. 'Relax, Laura. Use your intuition, make

some appointments and hear what your favourites have to
say.'

Solemn-faced to have such awesome responsibility, she
applied herself with a will and began to enjoy the task. Her
decision to enter every single applicant on a database had
been greeted with approval by Cassian and her fingers flew
over the keys as she entered the names and addresses.

'Time for lunch,' he murmured in her ear, seemingly a
few minutes later.

She checked her watch. 'It can't be that late!' she exclaimed.

'You've been working non-stop. Take a break.'

'I'd rather continue. Could we have sandwiches?' she
asked hopefully.

'I can do better than that.'

Cassian disappeared and returned later with smoked
salmon, pasta salad and two wicked cream cakes.

'Pastry on your mouth,' he drawled lazily, when they'd
finished. 'No, let me!' The tip of his tongue slid around her
lips, making her tremble. 'Tasty.'

'You're supposed to be the office boy today, so go and
make me an espresso,' she said haughtily, pretending she
wasn't feeling hot throughout her body.

'Mmm. Ever had a fantasy about an innocent young office boy being seduced by his glamorous, high-flying boss?'
he murmured, slipping his fingers to her zip at the back of
the honey-gold dress. 'Across her executive desk?'

Her eyes gleamed as her body capitulated. She walked
over to her desk and without taking her eyes off him,
hitched herself onto it, her skirt high on her thighs.

'Come and learn a little office practice, *boy*,' she purred
silkily.

She saw him swallow, knew he was hopelessly drawn to
her. Elated, she leaned back, unable to believe he found
her so enticing.

His mobile rang. He ignored it. And played the game to the full.

'Lunch hours have never been such fun,' she gurgled later, when they were mutually soaping one another in a haze of satisfaction. 'Enough!' she protested, when Cassian came dangerously close to arousing her again. *'Work.'*

Escaping, she pulled on her clothes and shakily returned to her lists. Time passed quickly again and it seemed only an hour or so before they were driving home. Somewhere in the depths of Cassian's pocket, his mobile rang.

'Can you answer that?' he asked.

'Yes, of course.' She dug it out. 'Hello?' she said uncertainly.

'Oh. Where's Dad?'

'It's Jai!' she squealed.

Cassian's eyes lit up like beacons. 'Can't stop here, too dangerous. See what he wants,' he urged.

'He's driving. Can I give him a message?' she suggested excitedly.

'OK. Can you tell him I'm sitting on the wall outside his house?'

Laura's eyes rounded. 'What? You've arrived? This is fantastic. He'll be over the moon—wait, oh, it'll be a good half hour or so before he can get to you—'

'No sweat,' said the composed Jai. 'I can wait.'

'See you soon,' she said happily. There was a casual 'OK' and then Jai rang off. 'He's there!' she told Cassian. 'At the house!'

'That must have been him, ringing earlier. I totally forgot to check if any message had been left. I can't wait for you to meet him. And Adam,' he said enthusiastically. 'We'll pick him up from school first.'

She beamed, thinking of them all together. Just like a family.

'I can't wait,' she replied.

*   *   *

The noise was deafening but she loved it. Jai had brought his father a tape of a local band playing in some market square in Marrakesh. Adam and Jai were excitedly chattering together, heads close, as Jai described the Berber houses in the mountains, where hospitality was so generous that he'd been overwhelmed by the excess of food and love. Cassian sat listening to the tape and occasionally adding to the stream of information coming from his son. His hand gripped Jai's, his eyes resting on his child with naked adoration.

And she was trying to get the meal together, having shooed away all offers of help, while at the same time she was doing her best not to miss a word of Jai's extraordinary tales of mountain passes, verdant valleys and ruined fortresses.

But mainly he spoke of the people. Her mind teemed with images and ideas, astonished that a ten-year-old boy should have experienced so much.

The vividly colourful clothes of the women, who worked in the fields and grazed the cattle and goats. The closeness of the families and the affection between them all. The remarkable fact that wherever they went, even in a remote valley, someone would appear. And that someone either spoke English or knew a villager who did.

She smiled, caught up in the excitement of Jai's arrival, thrilled to see how happy he was to be with his father. He was a handsome child. Dark, rangy, like Cassian, and clearly tough and self-assured. But sunny-natured, laughing a good deal, and never arrogant, never conscious that his life must be so different from most other children's.

Her eyes softened. She would never forget his meeting with his father. Cassian had leapt from the car as if ejected by a rocket. The two had flown together and had remained in a hug for ages; weeping, exclaiming, squeezing.

Without realising, her arm had gone around Adam too.

And she'd felt weepy when her son had cuddled her hard, his small face lifted to hers in love and happiness.

'Isn't life great now, Mum?' he'd said, starry-eyed.

'Great,' she'd agreed. And promised to herself that she'd do everything to keep it that way.

She hadn't stopped smiling since. Lifting the broccoli off the hot plate, she grinned at the laughing men in her life and coughed loudly to attract their attention.

'Supper's ready,' she announced, flushed pink from cooking and deep contentment. 'Jai, it's your choice. Eat here or the dining room?'

'Here, please!' cried Jai. 'It's smashing. Cosy and homely. Can we have candles?'

'I'll get them!' offered Adam, jumping up.

'I'll come too—'

The boys disappeared. Cassian looked up at her and if she hadn't fallen love with him before she would have done so then. There was such pleasure in every cell of his body and such exhilaration in his gleaming dark eyes that her heart somersaulted chaotically.

'He's wonderful,' she said shakily.

'I think so. I'm glad you do,' he replied.

He reached out his hand and she grasped it, both of them grinning idiotically at one another.

'I'd better put the meal on the table,' she breathed, afraid that she'd tell him how much she loved him. And she pulled her hand away.

'Crikey!' gasped Jai rushing in. 'Just look at that beef! Smells stupendous. I can't wait. I'm starving!'

Pleased, she began to carve. 'When did you last eat?' she asked in amusement, watching Jai pile potatoes and vegetables onto his plate.

'Umm… In Skipton, just before my minder put me on the bus.'

Adam giggled. 'I can't imagine what Skipton made of a

Berber in full ceremonial robes standing at a bus stop with you!'

'Did draw the crowds a bit,' Jai acknowledged. 'But Karim's got a degree in Psychology so he handled it. I love England, Laura. People are so friendly and smiley.'

'Are you sure?' she asked, a little astonished.

'I grin at them and they grin back,' Jai said blithely.

'I can imagine,' she said with a smile. He'd charm the birds off the trees. 'But we don't all have a tame Berber to help the conversation along.'

Jai laughed and sampled a piece of beef. 'Wowee, this tastes fab, Laura!' he declared. 'The absolute best!'

'Thanks,' she said warmly, won over by Jai's enthusiasm. 'I wondered what you'd think of the food in this country, after all the exotic stuff you've eaten.'

'But it's exotic here!' Jai claimed.

'Yorkshire?' hooted Adam.

Jai nodded. 'It is, to me. It's foreign. Exciting. I've never been to England before. Dad's talked about it a lot. In fact, he hardly ever *stops* talking about the Yorkshire Dales—'

'Exaggeration!' Cassian protested.

'In the last month or so, all I hear,' said Jai with the kind of affectionate scorn reserved for a wayward parent, 'is how beautiful it is, how green, the charm of the hills and trees and little fields and tiny villages. And do you know something, Dad?'

'I'm a bore?' he suggested.

Jai grinned. 'Never in a million years! No, you're right! This place blew me away. I know why you drooled about it.' He ducked to avoid an accurately hurled lump of bread. 'Seriously, though…is this going to be our home, now, Dad?'

'Could you really *live* here?' Adam cried hopefully, before Cassian could answer. But she saw he was frowning and a slight feeling of unease spread over her. 'We'd have a great time together,' Adam enthused.

'Yeah! Could you show me the corpse way you told me about?' Jai asked eagerly. 'And…what was it…Li'l Emily's Bridge? And the suspension bridge that wobbles and—'

'All of it!' broke in Adam. 'It's Saturday tomorrow, so I don't have school. We'll go early. And there are the remains of Roman lead mines above the village, and ruins of Victorian mining offices and a forge. It's dead interesting—'

'Dad!' Jai cried, his eyes shining. 'We can stay, can't we? Adam and me'll have a great time—'

He and Adam vied to coax Cassian. Laura suddenly couldn't eat. Her future—Adam's future—had been suddenly pushed to the forefront.

It had been obvious that Jai thought Cassian must be renting the house, as was his custom. She knew that he'd spent two years renting rooms in Morocco, two years in an Egyptian apartment before that, and a holiday home in Madagascar before then…

It puzzled her why Cassian hadn't explained he'd bought Thrushton Hall. Her eyes grew troubled. And she held her breath while he tried to make himself heard over the eager boys.

'I thought we'd stay for a while—' he began.

The boys whooped, waving their forks triumphantly in the air.

'Brill, Dad! Gosh, Laura, you don't mind?' exclaimed Jai.

'I—don't mind.' How could she? She adored him. And loved his father. 'I'd love to have you here,' she said warmly, aware that Cassian was frowning. But it was his own fault. He should have told Jai what he'd done.

Jai leapt from his chair and ran over, giving her a hug which left her breathless.

'It'll be like having a Mum around,' he said, misty-eyed.

'I've always wanted one of those but Dad wouldn't play ball!'

'Jai—' growled Cassian.

'It'll be like living in a real home, with a real Mum,' Jai said, not in the least bit unnerved by his father's ferocious scowl. 'I wish I had one. A Mum, I mean.'

'Is she dead?' asked Adam, with the typical bluntness of a child.

'When I was born. Dad said she was the most beautiful woman he's ever seen. I've got pictures of her, I'll show you. She was terribly clever. A novelist. He's never really got over her—'

'Jai!' muttered Cassian.

'Well, it's true, Dad! You told me you'd never love another woman, remember?'

Laura tensed, her stomach plummeting. This was awful. Could she ever make him forget this perfect wife, who'd tragically died before boredom or familiarity could set in? Who he remembered with rose-coloured spectacles?

'Yes,' Cassian said in a hoarse whisper. His face was unnervingly bleak. 'I remember.'

She felt sick. Cassian looked dreadful. He was carrying a torch for his late wife. Her hopes came crashing about her ears.

'Wish I had a father,' Adam put in, gazing significantly at Cassian, raw hope in his eyes.

She didn't know where to look. Her fingers trembled. The boys were voicing her dreams. Cautiously she stole a quick glance at Cassian. He was frowning at his plate, cutting up a piece of beef into increasingly small pieces.

'What happened to your Dad?' Jai asked gently.

'He didn't stand by Mum,' Adam said, his voice indignant. 'He left her in the lurch. But she's the best Mum in the world. You can share her if you like.'

'Can I?' Jai asked, his face wistful.

Laura's heart jerked painfully. 'Of course, Jai,' she husked. If Cassian would only let her…

'I thought you liked wandering the world, Jai,' Cassian said gruffly, still intent on dissecting the beef out of all existence.

'I do! It's cool!' Jai declared with passion. 'I love new places and getting my education first hand from you and where we are, instead of—'

'Wow! Your Dad teaches you?' Adam asked in awe.

'Yeah. Our life's too nomadic for me to go to school. Dad sets me work—like…doing the shopping in the souk, working out exchange rates, comparing prices and currencies in other countries, that kind of thing. Or…I do a study on the effect of land form and climate on people's lifestyles—that was my last project. Or local art—that's great, I get to talk to some real odd bods. And when Dad's finished writing for the day, we talk over what I've done.'

Cassian had stiffened imperceptibly. He was staring fixedly at the oblivious Jai—who was happily eating—as if he wanted to convey a message. Laura's eyes narrowed.

'Course,' Jai went on, prompting Cassian to tense up even more, 'when Dad's *really* motoring on a book, I have to create my own education. That's quite fun. I brush up on the local language or do a bit of painting. Sometimes I just read and read.'

Laura's mind was racing. Cassian's late wife had been a novelist. And he spent long hours 'motoring on a book'.

'I write thrillers,' Cassian said quietly, plainly reading the expression on her face. 'Under a pseudonym. I tell no one, *no one*, who I am. I don't like my private life invaded. We travel so that I can research a particular setting for a novel.'

'Wow!' Adam's eyes were popping. 'Are you famous?'

'I'll say!' Jai answered, matter-of-fact.

'But anonymous,' Cassian warned, and his son at last took the hint.

'We won't tell anyone. Will we, Adam?' Laura promised.

A writer, she thought. And if Jai hadn't innocently spilled the beans, she wouldn't have known. Even now, Cassian wasn't intending to tell her the name he wrote under. That hurt. He didn't want to share a huge part of his life with her. She felt suddenly flat and depressed. Where did she stand with him?

'You work on a computer?' she asked, remembering how he'd deflected her questions about his job.

His eyes begged her forgiveness for that evasion. 'I do.'

'Anyway,' Jai went on, 'it's a great way to live. I'm not knocking it, Dad. But for a while I'd like to be here. It's a super house, isn't it? And Adam and I are already good mates. Laura's my kind of Mum-substitute. I'd have chosen her out of a million other women—'

'Only a million?' Cassian asked, eyebrow raised.

'Ten,' Jai amended.

'A billion,' Adam said.

She waited for Cassian to make his contribution. An advance on a billion would have been nice. But he didn't.

'Jai, it's OK,' he said instead, quite unusually stilted in his manner. 'We're staying put for at least a couple of years. After then…I'm not sure. You know how it is.'

'Two years!' the boys crowed. Cassian opened his mouth and shut it, his jaw tight.

Laura almost joined in the cheers. She began to feel a little better, knowing that she had two whole years with Cassian. They'd live in close proximity. Judging by the way that they had instantly melded into a happy, friendly unit, they would all get on well. And Cassian would surely not want to break that unit up at the end of that two years.

Maybe she wouldn't ever be as special or as beautiful as his late wife, but she would be an important part of his life. And that was enough for her.

Serene amid the noisy, excited chatter, she smiled indulgently at the boys as their friendship blossomed.

'I'm shattered,' Jai announced with a yawn when they were all sitting in the drawing room around a cheery log fire. 'Mind if I go to bed?'

'Me too,' said Adam.

'I'll make up a bed,' Laura said warmly.

'Will I be in the same room as Adam?' Jai asked, his eyes so appealingly like Cassian's that she laughed, unable to resist his plea.

'If you like!'

She covered her ears when the boys shouted their delight and found herself enveloped in wiry arms, one dark head and one fair buried against her middle.

'I think you're a hit, Laura,' Cassian said in a thoughtful tone.

She heaved a huge sigh of pleasure and put away her niggling doubts about Cassian's love for his late wife.

'Has there ever been a more perfect day?' she marvelled, her eyes desperately hoping that he'd agree.

'It's been eventful,' he replied, with masterly understatement. 'Come on, boys. A quick bath each and bed. I'll tell you about the ghost of the miner's daughter who haunts Bardale Peak if you're tucked up in fifteen minutes.'

'Ten!' cried Adam and led the charge up the stairs.

Cassian followed Laura, his mind in turmoil. He could barely answer her comments as they moved the spare bed into Adam's room and made it up for Jai. He'd get through the next half hour and then he'd have to do some thinking.

She was humming to herself. Her entire face seemed luminous and he couldn't bear the pain that gave him.

'Adam will do so well, with Jai here,' she said softly, her eyes shining with happy tears. 'You...you don't know what this means to me, Cassian,' she continued. 'To see my child transformed, because of you, because he has found a trustworthy friend in Jai, means more to me than if I'd won the lottery.'

He understood. And because he did, because he knew that his own happiness depended largely on Jai's well-being, he felt doubly torn. She and Adam had changed beyond all recognition. Jai wanted them all to live like one big family.

And he...he even wished he could tutor Adam so the two boys learnt together. It was a fatuous idea. Of course it was.

'I'll chivvy those boys up,' he said shortly and knew she was disappointed that he hadn't acknowledged her happiness. She looked at him uncertainly and then went downstairs.

He stood in Adam's empty bedroom and gave a token yell at the boys, his breathing hard and fast. He couldn't allow this situation to develop. Nor did he want to feel this deeply. Didn't want to be possessed, obsessed.

His freedom was seeping away and soon he'd be back in the nightmare of his youth. Trapped. Cornered as surely as if he'd been shut in a cupboard.

The sex was fantastic. But love...that was something else. He didn't want this compulsion to stay close to Laura, to touch her every few moments, to ache with a sense of loss when she wasn't within his sight.

Love struck deep inside you. It took over your muscles, your veins, your lungs and every single brain cell. He would fight it. Stay detached.

'Story!' yelled Jai, hurling himself forwards like a projectile.

Cassian caught him and flung him on the bed, laughing despite his worries. And he did the same to Adam, because the child desperately needed some rough and tumble too.

God. What was he going to do, break three hearts?

CHAPTER ELEVEN

AFTER the story he told Laura that he had work to do, and went into the study, her image—soft, sensuous, loving—imprinted indelibly on his brain.

Of course he couldn't work. He couldn't think, either, and sat in a leather chair morosely nursing a whisky, wishing that life consisted of him and Jai and no one else.

Except…he sighed. Laura filled his mind, intruding on logical thought. Perhaps tomorrow he'd be more able to decide what to do. If the weather was suitable, he'd take a flight and let his instincts dictate his future.

Feeling extraordinarily tired and subdued, he wandered slowly along the darkened hallway to where Laura sat reading recipes in the sitting room.

The firelight cast a glow over her absorbed face. Her dark lashes were thick arcs on her flawless cheeks and her lips were parted as she frowned at the recipe book, perhaps, he mused, working out quantities or deciding which day she'd surprise them with another superlative meal.

But she was a meal in herself. Her lissom body was curled on the sofa, every inch of her desirable from the top of her gleaming scalp to the delicate, beautifully arched feet which he had kissed so fervently that very day.

Something hard and painful cramped in his chest and he bit back an urge to invite her to stay for ever. With a tremendous effort, he forced his voice to sound casual.

'I'm going up. Fantastic supper,' he said, extending his goodnight even though he wanted to hurry away to the isolation of his room. 'See you tomorrow. Night.'

She had risen, her eyes on his. He could turn away with

a curt nod... No. He couldn't. She held him fast, his feet were rooted to the ground.

'Goodnight,' she said softly, coming to put her arms around his neck.

He found himself kissing her, the sweetness of her mouth taking his breath away.

'I'm pleased Jai likes me,' she sighed, snuggling into his embrace more securely.

Unseeing, he stared over her head. Jai's longing for a mother had shaken him—together with the fact that his son had clearly wanted stability, too, a home of some kind.

The wanderer wants a home, he thought wryly. The homebody wants to wander.

'I've never kissed a famous author before,' she murmured into his throat. 'I suppose you're a literary genius and that's why you aren't rich beyond the dreams of Averil.'

He smiled at her joke. And felt safe enough with her, sure of her discretion, to come clean. He didn't want secrets from her. He wanted to share.

'I am rich,' he said gently. 'I just don't keep much of my money. It comes in, I keep what I think I'll need, and the rest—'

'Goes to the charity?' she gasped.

'I trust you not to breathe a word to anyone.'

Her hand lifted to caress his cheek. 'You are the most amazing man I've ever known,' she said shakily.

A wonderful sensation—pride, joy, contentment—meandered silkily through every inch of his body. 'You must get out more,' he chuckled. Kissed her small nose, and beat a hasty retreat.

With a crescent of Day-Glo orange spread out behind him, he checked the wind and cloud formations again. His narrowed eyes scanned the ridge of hills, now lit by the warm morning sun.

Tightening the strap on his helmet, he began the short run to the edge of the hilltop and launched himself into the air.

Freedom.

A huge sigh released itself from his tense chest. It was a long time since he'd flown and he'd missed the sensation of becoming unshackled from the world.

His feelings for Laura were more intense than any he'd ever known, but he had to remember that a permanent relationship came with strings that eventually strangled him.

Yet Jai would love to have her around.

Cassian searched for more lift, found it, and shot up a few hundred feet. Now he could see Thrushton and the manor at the edge of the village. What was it about this place that gave him such a sense of calm and well-being? It was as if he had come home—despite his troubled teenage years there.

Jai and Adam would be exploring Hangman's Wood by now. They'd come back, dirty, dishevelled and talking nineteen to the dozen and Laura and he would listen to their exploits and smile at one another...

He frowned. Laura. Laura, Laura! She never left him alone. Slid into his thoughts and his vision, forcing him to acknowledge how powerfully she had entered his life. Too far, too fast. He had to cool things down. And separation was the only way.

He'd never intended that she should stay. Jai and Adam and Laura had misinterpreted his remark when he'd said they'd be living at Thrushton Hall for at least two years. He'd been referring to Jai and himself. Now he'd have to clarify the situation.

No problem. A straightforward statement of fact. And yet he was shying away from even voicing it to himself.

Slowly he worked his way along the ridge in the direction of Thrushton, as though he couldn't bear to be parted from it for long. The wind began to buffet him and he had to stop thinking and focus hard on keeping up in the air.

But he was losing height and the wind was throwing him around too violently so he made a running landing and packed up for the day, feeling vaguely unsatisfied.

The flight had been enjoyable but it hadn't thrilled him as it used to. He found he was hurrying to fold up his 'wing', eager to return...to Laura.

He groaned. Maybe if he steeped himself in her the obsession would pall. He'd go back, make love to her... His body jerked in anticipation and he ruefully stowed the wing in its sack, recognising that there was only one thing on his mind. To hold Laura in his arms. To smell her, feel her, hear her, look at her.

The journey was short, he knew, but even then it took too long. And when he arrived, shouting to her, struck dumb by the answering silence, he knew a disappointment so keen that it unnerved him totally.

He'd wanted to see her smile at him, the cute lift of each corner of her lips, the whiteness of her even teeth. To listen to the warmth in her voice with its husky cadences as she spoke to him. Her scent was in his nostrils now, tantalising him; the clean smell of the shampoo she used, the subtle elusiveness of her favourite geranium and orange soap.

But without her presence, there was nothing but emptiness in the big house. It was as if it had died.

Quite at a loss as to what to do, he wandered into the garden behind the manor and passed the time waiting for Laura by planning a herb garden. It would be dual purpose—culinary and medicinal, and he'd draw on what he'd learnt from the Morrocan herbalist.

Mint to keep flies at bay. Nettles for pesticide—and to flavour the soft fruit he'd grow, chives for blackspot and aphids on the roses... Meadowsweet, heartsease, chamomile...

He couldn't wait to start planting. And what else? Per-

haps at the far end of the garden he'd build a chicken run
so they could have fresh, new-laid eggs. Extend the vege-
table garden of course—

He blinked, and leaned against the sunwarmed wall of
the house, suddenly sure—absolutely positive—that he
wanted to put down roots here. Not just for two years. For
the rest of his life. His mouth curved into a smile, his decision giving him a peace of mind he'd never known before.

'You look happy,' came Laura's soft voice.

It trembled a little, as if emotion bubbled within her and
her eyes were luminous. He felt his knees weaken.

'I am.' But he didn't tell her why. And he had to fight
his longing to include her in his plans.

'So am I. I've been talking to Tom about my mother.
It's so wonderful, getting to know her, Cassian!'

'I'm very pleased for you,' he said, lightly touching her
arm.

And suddenly she was nestled up to his chest and the
house, the garden, his life, seemed complete again. His lips
caressed her forehead while fear and excitement tussled
with one another.

Maybe his idea of sating his desire wasn't a good one.
It went without saying that Laura gave him the kind of
sexual satisfaction he'd dreamed about. But she also made
security and a cosy family life seem appealing. When, in
fact, it wasn't.

Her fingers laced in his hair. Her laughing eyes were
melting into his. Every part of his body was alight, ener-
gised, strangely empty. With increasingly drugged eyes, he
gazed at her soft lips and let her warmth seep remorselessly
into him. He paused, his heart thundering. There was nothing he could do to draw back—his desire was too overwhelming.

'I want you,' he said hoarsely.

Detaching herself, she gave a beguiling smile and walked

to the door, the glance over her shoulder telling him that he was to follow.

And follow he did, hopelessly tied to a woman's smile, soft blue eyes, a lushly mobile body. And hoping that was all. Pure physical lust.

Gently, with near-reverence, he made slow and adoring love to her. The poignancy of her whimpers and sighs caused a bitter-sweetness within him that led him to extend her pleasure until she was almost weeping with frustration.

His climax, and hers, both awed and unnerved him. Nothing could be this good. He was imagining it. No two bodies could move in such harmony, feel so good, offer such mutual rapture, or make him wonder if he'd been bewitched or transported to a heaven.

He didn't want to move, but held her in his arms, lost in a state of unbelievable bliss. And fear. This was getting beyond his control. No one should feel so attached to someone.

It was as if he depended on Laura for his very existence. A lump of terror came up in his throat, his heart beating frantically. And he finally detached himself.

They were both quiet when they wandered hand in hand downstairs later, and he wondered if she too was contemplating their relationship.

His throat dried again. He had to make his position clear. It was only fair.

'Laura,' he croaked, as she began her bread-making ritual. 'I must talk to you. Get things straight—'

'Things?' she asked, her eyes instantly wary.

He took the precaution of staring out of the window. Without her glorious, sexually glowing face in his vision, he'd focus more sharply.

'I think, over the past few days,' he muttered, 'I've known every emotion in the book.'

'Me, too.'

Hearing the smile in her soft voice, he steadied himself,

his hands flat on the work counter. Behind him he could hear the dough being thumped and he hurried on, anxious not to hurt her.

'It's…it's happened so fast, been such a roller-coaster that I hardly know where I am—'

'I know. It's lovely but it's scary, too,' she murmured in agreement.

'We need to slow down a bit.'

He almost smiled at himself. Was this really him talking—advising caution? Was he actually suggesting they lived with their heads for a while, instead of their instincts?

'If you like,' she said casually.

His head lifted in relief. She wasn't going to tie him down, to demand further commitment. A load lifted from his mind and he turned to watch her as she deftly kneaded the dough. Not too violently. Normal. Rational. Serene. And she smiled encouragingly at him, a dazzling smile that made his heart ache.

'I'm glad you feel that way,' he husked.

'I wonder,' she mused, glancing out of the window behind him, 'where Adam and Jai have got to now? They're as thick as thieves, aren't they?' She laughed, her pearly teeth glistening in her rosy mouth. 'I suppose I'll have a heap of washing to do when they come in!'

He knew what she was implying. That their sons were now a unit. But, he thought with a frown, that didn't mean they all had to live together.

'Laura, I don't want to lose what we have, you and me—'

'Nor do I,' she said, her eyes far too tender and mesmerising for him to stay unmoved.

'You know, I hope, that I'm not a man to make commitments,' he warned with quick urgency. 'I don't want to be trapped—'

'What commitments? And who's trapping you?' she asked in amiable surprise. 'You come and go as you like and I don't ask where you've been or where you're going—'

'It's not just that,' he said gently. 'Let me explain. You told me once that I wasn't to make Adam too fond of me because I wasn't going to be part of his life for long—no, wait, hear me out,' he said, when it seemed she'd interrupt.

The dough was left unheeded on the table. Dusted appealingly with flour as usual, she stared at him wide-eyed, her arms hanging by her sides.

'I'm listening.' Her voice shook.

'We're in danger here of giving the kids the wrong idea.'

'Are we?' she asked, her eyes piercing blue and startlingly luminous.

He could kiss her. Brush her hair from her forehead, chide her for coating herself in flour...

He swallowed. This had to be said. 'I'm worried that we're all getting too cosy. We're moving into Walton territory.'

'Nothing wrong with that, except all those interminable "goodnights",' she said with a wicked little grin.

No way could he smile. He was too worried. 'And what if it all goes wrong?' he shot. 'You saw how Jai was about you,' he croaked, longing to take her in his arms and say it would be all right, that she wouldn't be hurt. But he couldn't promise that. 'He wants a mother figure and has fixated on you. But the last thing I want is for him to be upset. We don't know what will happen between us, you and me. We might stay together for a while and part, we might separate tomorrow. Nothing is certain in this world. We can't let the boys think we're heading towards something permanent.'

He could feel the pain in her. And it was tearing him in two. But he had to be honest.

'You can't protect Jai from everything,' she breathed. 'You've taught me that. What happened to seizing the day? To living life? Learning to cope with disappointments?'

She wouldn't accept what he wanted, he thought with a slicing fear. Laura would want commitment. A husband, children—he'd always known that. She ought to be married to a loving man, not tied to someone who couldn't bear the finality of marriage. His spine chilled. Almost certainly he'd lose her.

And yet honesty and decency made him plough on, even though he knew he was heading towards a separation he'd find hard to bear.

'Jai is impulsive and passionate. He thinks you're wonderful. I'll be nagged to put our relationship on a firmer footing. I can't do that. I'm just suggesting that we can cool things and make this more of a friendly relationship, if we detach ourselves a little.'

'How do you suggest we do that?' she asked, widening her big blue eyes. She looked at him with a suspiciously provocative tilt of her head. 'I do find it hard not to touch you, Cassian. And we look at each other ten times a minute. The boys aren't stupid.'

He frowned. This wasn't going the way he'd planned. 'We'd be less…obsessed with one another if we didn't live together. I never wanted that,' he said with unintentional sharpness. And although he wasn't looking at her—but examining his shoes with intense interest—he knew she had stiffened. 'I said to Jai that we'd be here for two years but I think you all assumed that you and Adam would be part of that set up. Nothing was farther from my mind. You and Adam must live somewhere else. In the village, maybe—there are a couple of houses for sale, or Grassington—I'd buy a house for you both—'

'So I'd be your secret mistress,' she said, suddenly cold.

Alarmed that she was withdrawing from him mentally, he took a step forward. And she took one back. He felt panic welling up inside him.

'We'd have a relationship,' he corrected huskily. 'We'd

spend a good deal of time together, going out with the kids, reading them bedtime stories, that kind of thing—'

'And I'd pop over for sex. Or we'd use the back of your car. Or a convenient field.'

His breath rasped in. 'It's not like that—'

'Yes, it is.' She folded her arms and her eyes were as dark as a threatening storm. 'Just *you* get *this* straight. I won't be used as a substitute mother for your son and to satisfy your sexual demands!'

'Don't misinterpret what I'm saying! We both agree we're going too fast and need to find a way to put the brakes on. This would achieve that. Please don't think I'm using you. I want more than that—' he found himself saying desperately.

'What?' she shouted. 'To fall asleep beside me? To wake up and find me in your arms?' she cried, tormenting him with the passionate words he'd spoken earlier. 'So what do I do? Commute? Leap up at dawn and hurry home? Do I find a baby-sitter to stay in the house so Adam is safe? No, Cassian! I don't want to be at your convenience, at your beck and call. I deserve better. Either I live here with you, or we part. I mean *really* part. You choose. Now.'

He gazed at her in horror, his hand scraping distractedly through his hair. That wasn't what he'd wanted. Just something slower, less threatening to his freedom. He couldn't imagine what it would be like without her...

'I've not made myself clear,' he said, choked.

'Oh, yes, you have!' she raged. 'It's your late wife, isn't it? You think you can't love another woman because she was so perfect. Well I'm not filling her shoes. I have shoes of my own. I am not her. I am me. And if you don't want me as I am, warts and all, then have the grace to say so. But don't use me to assuage your guilt because Jai needs a motherly touch, and don't use me as a sex object for your voracious appetite! It's not fair on me! I want sex too. But I want a hell of a lot more than that from the man I give my body to! So decide whether you want me, flesh and blood and living and breathing—or your late, perfect, beautiful wife who's dead, Cassian, *dead*!'

'You've got it wrong!' he said harshly, grabbing her arms. She put her hands to his chest and pushed, but he resisted, ignoring the flour and dough that now marked his shirt and rushing straight into his explanation. 'My wife wasn't perfect! Not anywhere near!' he hissed, his face ferocious as he remembered, felt the wounds, the misery, again.

'You married her!' she shot.

'And don't I regret it! I fell for her because I was only eighteen and ruled by my hormones and thought sexual pleasure was love. She was four years older with a hell of a lot of lovers in her past and a whore's skill in arousing men. But she didn't have an ounce of tenderness in her entire body! She lured me into a hasty marriage because she was already four months pregnant by another man—*yes*! Pregnant!' he snarled, when Laura jerked in horror.

'Jai?!' she whispered, appalled.

'Exactly,' he muttered bitterly.

'But…he's so like you!' she gasped.

He nodded, sick with misery. 'His mother was dark-haired. Spanish. Hence the similarity. She was beautiful, yes, but only on the outside.' He raised a harrowed face as memories came thick and fast. 'I knew her to be cruel and vicious to animals and her behaviour towards them made me want to retch,' he muttered. 'She had no compassion for the elderly, or those who were less than beautiful, and she made fun of them, ridiculed them unmercifully. Maria was an absolute bitch. I *loathed* her for trapping me into marriage!'

'But she's dead, Cassian—!' Laura said, infinitely caring.

'No. She isn't.'

'*What?*' she gasped.

He felt drained, as if the lie had taken away something

precious to him. His integrity. His belief in honesty at all times.

'She didn't die. I lied to Jai,' he confessed hoarsely. 'I never wanted him to come into contact with her, to learn the kind of woman she was. She'd tried to abort him. Her own baby, Laura!' He thought of the world without his beloved Jai and his eyes pricked with hot tears. 'She didn't care about him. He was a burden, something vile to her, because he'd ruined her figure. When Maria gave birth she dumped the baby on me, then vanished. I never saw or heard of her again and it took years for me to get a divorce and to free myself from her. Jai is not my son but—'

Laura froze. There had been a sound behind her. Ice chilled her entire body. Cassian was staring in horrified disbelief at something…someone…over her shoulder. And she knew before she turned who it must be.

CHAPTER TWELVE

IT WAS Jai. Dirty and dishevelled from his adventures outside. Looking suddenly small and pathetic, his mouth open in an O of despair, his eyes, his deceptively Cassian-like eyes dark and glistening with utter horror.

And then Jai gave a terrible shuddering cry like that of a wounded animal and he'd turned, lurching away in a sobbing frenzy before either she or Cassian could move their paralysed limbs.

'*Jai!*' he jerked out, in a horrific, broken rasping sound.

Automatically she whirled around, her hands lifting to stop Cassian from following. He cannoned into her, carrying her along a pace or two before he'd grabbed her to prevent them both falling over.

'No,' she said urgently. 'Not you.'

Pain etched deep in his face, his pain hurting her, knifing her through and through as if she was being stabbed over and over again.

'He's my son!'

His eyes squeezed tight as if he recognised the irony of that cry. And she felt the tears welling up in her own eyes and fought them. For his sake, for Jai, she must stay strong.

'He ran *from* you, not *to* you,' she said, as gently as she could. 'Let me go. Give us a while together.'

Without waiting for his reply, she flew into the hall where a bewildered Adam stood, his face as grubby as Jai's.

'Where did he go?' she demanded fiercely.

'Sitting room,' Adam cried. 'But what...?'

She hurtled in there. Nothing.

She bit her lip, wondering if he'd clambered out of the open window. But when she ran to it, she could see no sign

176

of him. Panic made her shake. The child would be so hurt.
His world had come crashing down, all the fantasies he'd
woven about his mother, the images he'd had of her; lovely,
loveable, kind...

And then she heard a stifled, muffled sob. She blanched.
It had come from the cupboard.

'Where's he gone?' rasped Cassian from the doorway.

She couldn't answer. But he read her appalled gaze and
flinched. Her hand stayed him. Quietly she stepped close
to the door and laid her hand on it as if consoling the child
within Cassian's long-ago prison.

'Jai,' she said tenderly. 'It's me. Laura.' Her fingers
closed on the latch and gently eased it up. But the door
was locked. Jai had locked himself in from the inside with
the key Cassian had so carefully fitted in the lock. Her eyes
closed at the pity of it all. 'Don't cry, sweetheart,' she
crooned, love and compassion in every breath she uttered.

The dam burst; from behind the heavy panelled door, she
heard a storm of weeping. Anxiously she glanced around.
Adam was holding Cassian's hand, his young eyes aghast
at the bleakness of Cassian's face.

She had to make things right. She loved Cassian so much
that she'd do anything to stop him from hurting so badly.
Her hand waved Adam and Cassian back, indicating they
should retreat from the room.

'No one's here but me,' she said to Jai. She imagined
him, sitting on the cold stone floor, sobbing his heart out.
It was hard for her to keep her voice steady because she
was so distressed. 'Don't stay in there alone, Jai,' she
coaxed. 'Come and cuddle up with me on the sofa. Let me
hold you. Just that. Nothing more. And we can talk if you
want, or just sit together. Trust me. I know what it's like
for you. I heard terrible things about my mother that broke
my heart. Come to me. I understand. I've been there too.'

There had been a lessening of the wild crying whilst she
spoke and she knew he'd been listening. She held her

breath in the long silence that followed her plea. A stray
sob lurched out from Jai and then there came the sound of
scrabbling, as if he was standing up. Quietly she stepped
back. The key rasped and the door opened a fraction.

'Cassian isn't here,' she said softly. 'Just me.'

Around the edge of the door, a wrecked face appeared,
the small features screwed up in misery, the dark hair
shooting in all directions as if he'd thrust violent fingers
through it.

Heartbroken, she opened her arms and with a moan Jai
stumbled into them.

'There,' she murmured, guiding him to the sofa. 'Come
on. Snuggle up. I'll hold you tight. Cry if you want. I'm
waterproof.'

She stroked the weeping child's turbulent curls, her arms
securely around him. He clung to her like a limpet and she
occasionally kissed his hot forehead, waiting patiently until
his tears had subsided. It was a long wait.

'My m-mother was a cow!' Jai wailed. 'She…she didn't
want me—'

'But Cassian did,' Laura gently reminded him.

'No! He was lumbered with me!' Jai sniffed.

'You know that's not true.' Laura kissed his wet temple
and brushed soggy clumps of hair from the furrowed forehead. His tears seemed to have got everywhere, carried on
frantic hands. Poor sweetheart. 'Cassian is crazy about you.
He really believes you are his son in every way except by
blood. He's prouder of you than perhaps he ought to be.
The sun definitely originates from your person,' she said
with a gentle smile.

'I have a vicious tramp for a mother and an unknown
father!' Jai's appalled eyes gazed moistly into her own,
seeking comfort.

'That is awful for you,' she acknowledged gravely. 'I
thought I was in exactly the same situation as you, once,
so I do know how painful it is when your parents turn out

to be less than perfect. I was lucky. I discovered that my mother had been maligned and she wasn't horrible at all. My father too. I can't pretend that your mother was really a saint. But maybe she was scared because she was pregnant and unloved. People do terrible things when they're frightened, Jai. They seek self-preservation—think of themselves. That's how the human race is programmed when there's danger about.'

She shifted him more comfortably on her lap, gently wiping his tear-channelled face now that he'd stopped crying.

'Perhaps your father didn't know your mother was pregnant. Perhaps your mother has regretted leaving you, and you are never far from her mind. We can't ever be sure. But there is one thing we do know.'

'What's that?' Jai mumbled, sweetly grumpy.

Her lips touched his soft cheek. 'Cassian loves you,' she said, her voice shaking with passion. 'You are the most important thing in his life. Few people have such love. That makes you very special, very fortunate.'

'He *lied* to me!' Jai railed, screwing up his fists in anger.

'I know,' she agreed, soothing him with her gently stroking hands. 'And that only shows how much he cares. Cassian doesn't lie as a rule. It's a matter of principle to him. He's always honest—sometimes uncomfortably so,' she said, sadly rueful. 'But for you he made an exception. He couldn't tell you the facts about your mother. Perhaps he might have done, when you were older, but you wanted her to be wonderful, didn't you? So he invented a mother you'd adore. And we don't know how much it hurt him to keep up that pretence, how hard it must have been to say that his ex-wife was a paragon of virtue when she had hurt him and deceived him so badly. Do you understand why he felt compelled to lie to you, Jai?' she asked anxiously.

Cassian, listening in silent anguish from behind the door, his hand crushed by Adam's bony grip of sympathy, held his breath. He was nothing without his son. Without Laura.

'Yes,' he heard his son whisper.

Heard Laura murmur something, knew she was hugging Jai, rocking him. He threw back his head and closed his eyes, swamped by relief and gratitude. And admiration. By her tact and loving heart, she had given him the gift of his son. And for that, he could never thank her enough.

She was… He searched for a word to describe her but found nothing that expressed his feelings. More than wonderful. More than compassionate and caring. Selfless, tender, utterly sweet and loveable…

'You OK?' whispered Adam, stretching up on tiptoe to get close to Cassian's ear.

Dimly he saw the blond child's anxious face, saw the same concern and love that Laura displayed so openly. Unable to speak, he nodded, swallowing, and received a friendly squeeze of his mangled hand in response.

'Shall we see if we can call your father in?' he heard Laura say.

'Mmm,' snuffled Jai.

Adam beamed up at him. Laura's smile.

God, he loved her!

'Cassian!' she shouted. 'Are you around?'

He couldn't move. He was rooted to the ground in shock. He loved her so much that his lungs had lost their power and his heart seemed to have stopped beating.

Because he had messed up. He'd been so blind—had feared for his freedom so much—that he'd offered to keep her like some mistress, *like a caged bird*—to appear at his bidding, to make his life complete on his terms.

'Cassian!' she yelled, and Adam tugged at his hand urgently.

Laura wasn't like Maria. She would never trap him. She'd respect his need for space. And suddenly he didn't want that space so badly—he wanted her, to be with her, to be here in the manor and bathing in the warmth of her. Cooking breakfast, doing homework with the boys, explor-

ing the moors, developing the garden…but all with Laura.
With her in his heart. With her loving him.

Distraught, he obeyed Adam's desperate tugs and
Laura's calls. Like an automaton he walked stiffly to the
door, everything a blur because of the tears of despair in
his eyes.

'Oh, *Dad*!' Jai wailed.

A body hurled itself at him. His son in all but blood,
every inch, every bone as familiar to him as his own. Now
Adam, too, was hugging him. And someone…the smell of
Laura came to him. Laura. She was drawing them all forwards.

He felt the back of the sofa against his calves and found
himself being pushed down. The misery was so intense that
he couldn't respond to his son's desperate apologies but
eventually he realised how upset Jai was and he managed
to put on a show of normality.

'No, I'm fine. Just got a bit emotional,' he said huskily.
'I love you, Jai, Never want to hurt you. I'm sorry—'

'No sweat, Dad. I understand. Laura explained. I'm OK
about it. Honest. I've got you, that's the important thing.
And now we've got Laura. She's what I dreamed of when
I imagined my Mum.'

His son's face swam before his eyes. He couldn't say
that Laura was about to leave their lives. It wasn't the time.
But his heart felt as heavy as lead despite his cranked-up
smile. And he knew he had to be alone to grieve for his
lost love.

'Yeah. Great. Now how about you two getting off me so
I can breathe and flinging your grotty selves into a bath?'
he growled. 'You're a disgusting colour, both of you. Have
you been mud-wrestling or something?'

The boys giggled and leapt up. Jai hesitated, then bent
down to kiss him.

'Love you, Dad,' he said shakily.

'Love you, Jai,' he croaked.

And then there was the sound of elephants stampeding up the stairs, the sound of yells, water running...

'Cassian.'

Laura's voice, soft and gentle. Her hand stealing into his. What a fool he'd been. Freedom wasn't in being alone, doing your own thing. It depended on many factors.

It was like flying. He could only stay aloft if the wind was right, if the thermals were there, if he manoeuvred his wing properly—and if the wing was undamaged.

To be free he needed a base from which to fly. Somewhere secure and familiar. And he needed to be nurtured by the right person if he was to truly soar up into the heights of joy.

He drew in an agonised breath. He needed to be loved.

'I'm sorry, Laura,' he rasped.

'For what?' she murmured.

'Coming here.'

He couldn't look at her. Not that he'd see her if he did. The tears which he'd not shed through all the bullying, all the terror and desperation, were betraying him now and falling freely down his face. What would she think of him?

He struggled to control himself, to find his iron will. He'd need it. God, he'd need it in the next days, weeks, months.

'How do you mean?' she asked, not moving a muscle beside him.

'If I hadn't come—'

'I would still be a mouse,' she said. 'I wouldn't have a wonderful job. Adam wouldn't know how much I love him.'

'OK. Some good has come out of it,' he granted.

She watched him struggling and longed to help him. But stayed quiet. Patience, she told herself. All would be well.

'I think it would be better for us all if—after a decent interval—I left. You and Adam can stay in the house.'

'Oh.' She thought for a moment. 'Can I take in lodgers?' she asked with apparent gravity.

'Lodge…?' He scowled. 'Suppose so. It'll be your house.'

'And…' Risking all, she said quietly, 'If I fall in love. Would you mind if my lover came here?'

His teeth drove hard into his lower lip. She could feel all his muscles tightening till they were rigid and quivering from tension.

'Your house. Your decision,' he clipped.

His distress, his pain, spurred her on.

'So,' she whispered, snuggling up close. 'When are you moving in?'

For a moment or two she thought he hadn't heard. Not a breath lifted his chest, not a flicker of his eyes betrayed the fact that he was a living man and not a frozen statue.

'What…did you say?' he whispered, desperately trying to focus. He dashed his hand across his eyes and her heart turned over.

'I do love you,' she said, stroking his harrowed face. 'I think you love me. And I want to be with you. I don't care how long that might be. I want you to be free—'

His mouth descended on hers in a hard and impassioned kiss. He was moaning, muttering words of love and delight, saying how deeply he felt and that he wanted to be with her for the rest of his life.

'You mean everything to me,' he said passionately, holding her shoulders and staring intently into her eyes. 'I can't imagine life without you. With you, it's a miracle. An amazing feeling of serenity and exhilaration. Every part of my heart and mind and soul is filled with love for you. I adore you, Laura. Worship you.'

'Whoopee! I've got a Mum!' yelled Jai from behind them.

'I've got a Dad!' crowed Adam.

She and Cassian smiled ruefully at one another. 'And we've got gooseberries,' she giggled.

'I think,' Cassian whispered, 'we'll get the gooseberries fed and up to bed and have a little party of our own down here.'

'Whooooo*oo*!' the boys chorused.

Laura blushed. And turned to the towel-draped boys, her eyes full of love and amusement.

'Go away, you horrible children!' she laughed.

Jai and Adam looked at each other in resignation. 'Huh. Parents,' Jai pretended to grumble. And they scampered upstairs again, screeching with joyous laughter.

Cassian hugged her. 'Rascals,' he said fondly. Then he caressed her cheek. 'I've never been so happy,' he said roughly. 'Not in the whole of my life.'

'I think you might be,' she purred. 'After chocolate torte for supper. And after that...'

The love in his eyes touched her heart. Wonderingly, she reached up and touched his mouth. Then she lifted her face to his and lost herself in his kisses. Now she was truly, deeply happy. And all her dreams were on their way to coming true.

She sighed and sank deeper into Cassian's arms. Perfect love. Perfect lover. She was, without doubt, the luckiest woman in the world.

'Marry me,' Cassian whispered. 'Be my wife. I want that more than anything. I want us to have children. More gooseberries,' he said with a laugh.

Her face was radiant, her eyes sparkling like a bright blue sea beneath a blinding sun. 'I would love to be your wife,' she said shakily. She giggled. 'And to have your gooseberries!'

Cassian gave a shout of laughter and kissed her passionately.

'About time! Thought he'd never ask,' came Jai's stage whisper from the doorway.